Betrayal of the Heart

Queen Starasia

authorHOUSE®

AuthorHouse™
1663 Liberty Drive
Bloomington, IN 47403
www.authorhouse.com
Phone: 833-262-8899

Published by AuthorHouse 11/08/2023

ISBN: 978-1-4490-7443-2 (sc)
ISBN: 978-1-4490-7444-9 (e)

Library of Congress Control Number: 2010900357

Print information available on the last page.

Any people depicted in stock imagery provided by Getty Images are models, and such images are being used for illustrative purposes only. Certain stock imagery © Getty Images.

This book is printed on acid-free paper.

DEDICATION

First I have to thank my creator. You have blessed me with this talent to share with others.

To my children Ta'Quan, Sha'Quana, and Shallah.
Everything I do is all for you.

To my parents Thedra and Jerry Cunningham S.R.
Thanks for all that you have done for me.

To my sisters Tanaka and Tamara thanks for the Encouragement and faith.

To my only brother Jerry Cunningham J.R. also Known as Dela "Shot @ 3 (True Story) & SUN B.E.A.R. of BEAR SQUAD ENT. Keep doing Your thing! Paralyze Muzik for life.

Rest in Peace
Louise "COOT" Adams
Elix "COON" Adams
Deacon Major & Sister Frances Cunningham
Love Always daughter of a Cunningham

Thanks to Author's Publishing Company for giving me the chance to put my work out there. To all my family and friends thanks for the Support.

CHAPTER 1

On June 14, 1979 Tashione just turned 32 years old. She and her friends were celebrating it to the fullest. Tashione boyfriend asked `did she want another drink? Yes-said Tashione. While he was at the bar, he ordered a Gin & Juice for Tashione. Once he came back, sat down, said here you go baby, gave her a kiss, and said Happy Birthday baby. The next thing Tashione remember was a bunch of her friends crowding around her with a big ass cake singing the Birthday song to her. Tashione blew the candles out and Raul asked her to dance. After dancing off two songs, Raul wanted to sit down. Tashione was so messed up that she felt like her body was in a trance, and could not do shit. Tashione started to reminisce about her past when she first started drinking, smoking weed, and cigarettes. She could not believe that she started at the age 10 years old. Growing up in the city as a child, she had access to a lot of shit that she should not have access to. Tashione parents left her and siblings home with their Uncle Ron one Saturday night so they celebrate their 30th Anniversary. Once they left, Tashione got her weed together and ask could she go to the store and chill with her friends. Uncle Ron said sure, as long as you take your little sister Amise with you. Tashione said cool because Amise was not anything but a year younger than she was. They went to the store got a white owl cigar and a 40 ounce of Old English. Once they reached the back of the building Tashione rolled up the blunt and started smoking while Amise watched on at first. Can I try it Tashione? At first she just looked at her then gave it to her to try. Amise started too choked on it and Tashione took the blunt back. They started to walk toward the hang out spot know for the Juice Crew. Tashione introduce Amise to everybody then Boo came up to Tashione and said what is up baby girl? Just Chilin Boo! Boo wanted Tashione really bad, but that would never happen because Tashione was still a virgin. They all started lighting blunts. Boo handed Amise one and she took a pull and passed it on. Tashione looked at her watched seen it was almost 10:00 p.m. and knew it was time to get Amise back home. Tashione told Amise to come on so they can get home. As soon as they walked out Sha called out and said hold up Tashione I will walk you. They were walking and talking about them being together. Sha was telling Tashione that he loved her and hate being away from her. Tashione stopped walking and looked up at Sha smiling and gave him a kiss, not paying much attention to who was around. Tashione broke the kiss and said I love you as well and I am ready to take our relationship to the next level. Out of nowhere, here comes Boo Sha's friend. Boo had a gun saying no! She is mine and sha tried to pull Tashione behind him but boo was getting ready to fire the gun on her sister. Sha ran in front of Amise and caught the bullet in his right arm. Tashione started screaming and Boo ran. Tashione never seen so much blood in her life. She heard nothing at first and then she grabbed Sha to see if her sister was hurt. Amise was ok and then got up running toward Tashione for comfort. Sha got up and told Tashione to take him home now. Once they got there, Sha family was getting ready to take him to the hospital and Tashione eased out and headed home. Once Tashione got amise in their room she made Amise promise to keep her mouth closed about what happen. Tashione stayed close to home for a while until Sha came by looking for her. Tashione was asking Sha all kinds of question about the gun wound and did they find Boo? No, they did not find him yet and I do not want you to be out by yourself either Tashione. Sha pulled her in his arms and just held her while she cried on his shoulder. Sha told Tashione that he had something for her and she got all excited till Sha pulled out a short hand 9mm gun. Tashione did not know anything about guns; but Sha said he would teach her everything she needed to know. Every weekend they would practice in an old empty building until he felt Tashione knew how to shoot it good. Sha made Tashione promise to keep the gun with her at all times. Tashione done just what Sha told her to do. Tashione took the gun to school, shopping stores, clubs or just to hang out. One Saturday night Sha came to chill with Tashione and her family out of nowhere Boo came out and shot Sha in the back and the bullet came out of his chest. Tashione pulled her gun out and shot Boo in the chest until he fell down. Tashione grabbed Sha and was holding him in her arms rocking back and forth. Sha died in her arms. After Sha's death, Tashione was not the same anymore. She did not care about anything no more. She cut school and got into fights everyday until she finally was expelled from six different schools in one year. Tashione even got more involved in gangs. She manage to get into a gang called LAC Posse which ranged from kids around 9-21 of age and the leader was called Jazzy Tee. He was light skin and very sexy. Jazzy Tee wanted Tashione as his Queen so he played the very friendly roll to her for a while then one day he asked her to become his Queen. He told her the only way that could happen was to fight for it. Tashione was shock as hell but she said okay. Tashione asked Jazzy Tee whom she had to fight. Then a girl named Wendy came off the front porch standing all tall and fierce. Tashione was feeling scared but when she felt her gun on the side that feeling went away very quick. Everybody was forming a circle around him or her and they were sizing each other up. The other gang member was yelling for Wendy to get her but Jazzy Tee never said a word just watching Tashione. She turned to look at him and he winked his eye and said I want you for my Queen. Wendy got a sucker punch in while Tashione was looking at Jazzy Tee. Tashione went for what she knew. She grabbed Wendy by the neck and was choking her out. Wendy was trying to get Tashione hands off her but she could not the grip was locked. Wendy was going out for the count but Tashione did not know if the girl was out or just faking so she let go. Wendy came up behind her and put her in the chokehold with a knife to Tashione neck saying you are dead bitch! Tashione felt for her gun and pointed it to Wendy stomach and pulled the trigger. Wendy fell and Jazzy Tee was saying yeah I like that shit. Jazzy Tee said welcome my New Queen and Tashione went straight to his arms. Some of the gang member took Wendy to the hospital after the fight. The ones that stayed was Chilin outside in front of Jazzy Tee building smoking a blunt while Tashione was sitting between his legs. Keith passed the blunt to Tashione and right when she was about to puff it Jazzy said do not smoke that! Tashione was confused and just looked at him. Jazz told her I meant what I said do not smoke that shit. Tashione was getting mad and asked why? When jazz did not answer her, she started puffing the blunt. Jazz slap the shit out of Tashione and she grabbed her gun and pointed it right at his chest. Tashione told Jazz…"If you ever put your hands on me, to hurt me I will kill you where you stand." Jazz nodded his head and Tashione put the gun down. Jazz told Tashione that he just wanted to see if she was scared of him. Tashione told him as long as you put your pants on one leg at a time I will never be scared of you. They all continued smoking on a blunt. Tashione sister Amise walked up and told her she was needed at home immediately. Tashione got up kissed Jazz and said I will see you later. When they got home, there was not any real emergency that really concerned her. Tashione oldest sister Imani had gotten pregnant and they were having a family discussion. Tashione went to her room to find her sister crying on the bed. Tashione called Imani name but she did not respond. Tashione got on the bed and hugged her sister while she cried. Everybody knew that these two sisters never got along, but they were always there when one needed the other. (Present) Tashione came back to reality when her boyfriend asked her was she ready to leave and go home. Tashione looked at Raul smiling and said yes lets say goodnight to everybody. Once that was all done, they headed for the car. Raul opened the car door and Tashione got in then himself. When they arrived home Raul helped Tashione out of her clothes then put her to bed and chilled for a minute until she fell off to sleep. Raul eased out of the bed and changed his clothes and left out on his motorcycle. Benita was stumbling down the walkway when someone grabs her real quick and slit her throat. The next morning they both were wakening up to some loud banging on the door. Raul was the first to get to the door and asked who is it? It's the police open up! Raul opens the door and they asked for Ms. Jefferson. When Tashione came to the door, she was in his robe and had sleep still in her eyes when she told them to come in. The officer told Tashione that they found her friend Benita dead in her walkway. Tashione could not believe that someone killed her best friend and started crying while Raul hugged her. The police officer asked several questions before they left her their cards. Raul showed them out and went back to Tashione who was crying. He pulled her in his arms and held her while she cried. He asked her to stop crying because God has her now and will take good care of her. Tashione decided to go back to bed and rest up some more. At first Tashione could not sleep but after awhile sleep found her, and she started to dream. (Past) Tashione, Benita, and Amise was cutting school and getting high off some banana acid papers. They ended up on the roof of the school. Tashione was really fucked up because she took the most and started tripping real bad. She got real close to the edge and leaned over a little to far and almost fell off the roof, but Amise grabbed her arm in time. They all agreed to leave and go to Highland Park to meet up with Jazz and some of the LAC Posse. Once they got there, Jazz was upset about something and started yelling at Tashione about her being late and high as hell. Tashione looked at Jazz and said fuck you! You do not own me motherfucker! I do as I please! Before she knew it, Jazz had slapped Tashione so hard that her lip was busted and bleeding. She grabbed her gun and Jazz started to running while Tashione open fire on him. Everybody fell to the ground and a bullet grazed his leg and he fell. Everybody started running toward Jazz and Tashione bent down and pointed the gun in his face telling him next time I will not miss. Benita told Jazz please do not put your hands on her; you know she do not like that. Keith helped Jazz up and we all acted as if nothing happen. It was around 2:30 p.m. and time to head for home cause school was about to let out. Jazz called Tashione over to him and said I will never hit you again and I am sorry. Tashione had a look in her eyes like she could see right through him. Jazz told Tashione that she had the most evil, coldest look in her eyes but he still loved her now and forever and never change. Once Tashione got home, she acted as if she had homework. Her stepmother Rose knew she was lying because the school had called the house. Rose stepped in Tashione room and asked how school was? Tashione felt that her mom knew but decided to play along. I am trying to do homework! Rose said what homework child? I know you cut school because they called. That shocked look she gave her mother told it all so Rose said I'm taking your radio away from you for two week till you get your act straight. Tashione started yelling at her stepmother saying "you can't do me like that I love my music ma." Take anything else but the radio. Rose said no baby the radio and I will let your father know I took it from you. Tashione threw the books down and stomped her way out of the house headed for LAC Posse hang out on Alabama. Once she got there the other girls was getting ready to go shopping in Brownsville. Tashione asked Jazz for some money he reached in his pocket and pulled out a knot of money giving her five hundred dollars and then asked for a kiss. Tashione said thank you and gave him a kiss. The girls left and right when they cross the bridge a group of girls was at the end of it. Everybody looked at each other and told Tashione to be cool but the girls knew some shit was about to jump off. By the time they reached the bottom, one of Brownsville girls said you on the wrong side of town. Wee-Wop was the oldest so she told them Hell No!! All hell broke loose and the fighting begins and shit just got out of control. That is when Tashione pulled her gun out and started shooting in the air. Everybody stop and one of the girls from Brownsville named China snuff Tashione and she pop the girl in her hand because she was trying to block the bullet. Wee-Wop, Van and Tiny all flipped on Tashione because she was always shooting people. Instead of them shopping, they headed back home. When the girls got around the corner, the LAC boys knew something was wrong because there were no bags. Jazz asked Wee-Wop what happen. In addition, when she told Jazz he held out his hand for the gun. Tashione did not want to but she did and he went off on her. Tashione did not back down from him either and that really made Jazz mad. He wanted to beat her ass because of that sassy ass mouth but he knew if he hit her that he would have to kill her to stop her. They were all just hanging out and getting high when a cream color car drove by shooting. Everybody took cover; Jazzy covered Tashione body with his to make sure she was not hit. Wee-Wop caught a bullet in her thigh but everybody else was ok. Jazz grab Tashione and told her no more guns! Tashione could not see herself without one and she would not be without one either. The LAC Posse walked Tashione home and waited for Jazz to say good-bye. Tashione went straight to her building and took the stairs to her door. Once she opened the door and went in everybody was sitting around the table eating dinner. Her father said, oh look Rose it is our long lost child Tashione finally made it home. Tashione sucked her teeth and went in the bathroom to wash her hands and join them at the table. Divine was watching everybody eat because he was ready to leave so he could get back to his Atari game. Gene said if everybody is done, you can leave except Tashione. Everybody got up and Rose told Gene talk not yell. She got her plate and went to the kitchen to do dishes. Tashione was so fucked up she was not in the mood for her father lectures. She had put the visine in her eyes to take the redness away before she went home so she was straight. Once Gene got started he made the comment that he knew she was high and been drinking as well. Tashione spit kool-aid all over the table and looked at her father. Gene said okay Tashione since you want to smoke and drink like a grown up I want you to smoke these. He pushed a box that had five fat cigars in them. Gene told Tashione that if she smoked all five she had permission to smoke. Tashione thought it was cool because all she had to do was just puff but the joke was on her; she had to inhale as well. Tashione was okay at first but once she made it to the third one, she begins to feel sick on her stomach. She wanted to smoke so she done it and Gene gave her a fresh pack of Newport's.

CHAPTER 2

(PRESENT) Tashione jumps up from her sleep to feel the heat from the fire. She runs out of the bedroom straight to the front door. Her neighbor had already called the police and the fire station. Once they got there, they put the fire out and told Tashione that the bedroom had the most damage but your insurance should cover it. Tashione went in the house and called Soul and Necey to let them know what happen and she would be staying with her until her bedroom was fixed. By the time, she got to Soul house Tashione beeper was going off and it was Raul. Soul opens the door and took Tashione bag and hugged her very tight and they went in. Tashione asked her where the telephone was so she could call Raul to let him know what happened and where she was at. While she was talking to Raul, he was acting like he did not give a fuck about what happen or where she was at. Tashione thought it was weird but brushed it off. Soul told Tashione that she did not like Raul because it was something about him that gave off bad vibes. Tashione said okay let us burn one and cut the music on and they did. Tashione was dancing by herself off "To much buttie in the Pants." After the song went off Soul said, she was going to bed and would see her in the morning. Tashione was sitting in the living room and started thinking of the times she got into trouble and her mother Rose always got her out of it. (Past) Tashione dozed off and started dreaming about when she went shopping in Brownsville and out of nowhere a girl swung a steel bat at Tashione knees making them bleed and sending her to the ground screaming. All of the LAC Posse girls rushed over and lifted her up heading home to Jazz place. Once they got there and inside Mom-du were trying to clean her wounds and Tashione was cursing and yelling that it hurts please stop. Jazz heard her yelling from his window and told Keith that something is wrong with Tashione. He race up the stairs to his apartment and open the door Tashione was screaming Jazz name. He went to her and lifted her up in his arms telling her it was going to be okay. What happened to her knees? When they were done, explaining Jazz said she needs to go to hospital she

8

freaked out saying hell no! Please do not make me go Jazz. Jazz knew she needed to go and get stitches. With Tashione cutting up the way she Jazz paid cash money so she could see the doctor. They took x-rays and after everything was done, Tashione needed stitches but she was scared to death of needles. She would not even go for that, but Jazz told the Doctor to try it but he doubted it would work. When they entered the room where Tashione and Mom-du was at, Tashione was already saying Hell No! The Doctor told her that she needed the stitches. Out of the question Doc! Just wrap it up and send me on my way. Everybody gave up so the Doctor cleaned the wound and wrapped both knees up and said I want to see her in two weeks. They got home around 7:00 p.m. and Jazz laid Tashione in his bed and sat down right besides her moving her hair away from her face. Jazz said Tashione you know you stay in the most shit for you to be the baby girl of the Posse and the Queen. I want you to give up the guns and the gang to be with just me only. Tashione said what are you talking about? I am with you and only you. Jazz looked Tashione in her eyes and said I love you Tashione and I do not want to lose you to nothing or nobody. I want us to be together forever have us a couple of babies and get married when you is ready. Tashione told him she loved him as well, but she was still a baby herself but when she got out of school they could start a family after they was married. Jazz agreed and he wrapped his arms around her and said I love you. Jazz looked at his watch and said it time for you to go home baby. He helped her up and carried her to his car and headed for her house. Jazz helped her as much as he could to her door then she kissed him and told that she loved him and would call him later. Jazz left and she went in and struggled to her bedroom. When she lay on the bed she had broken out in a sweat, she hides her pain and wounds from everybody in her family. After a month went by, she was straight and never went back to doctor. Saturday rolled around and Tashione went to Jazz house, which she knew he was not up but she would just crawl in the bed with him. When she got there she was right and Jazz pulled her down and put his arm around her and said I love you and fell back to sleep and so did she. Mom-du came in the room to check on the two lovebirds, seen that they both was asleep and went right back out. Jazz woke-up first watching her sleep with a pacifier in her mouth. Jazz thought she looked so cute and peaceful. He eased out of bed and grabbed the camera snapping pictures of her sleeping with a pacifier. Jazz put the camera down and pulled the pacifier out and Tashione woke up and smiled. Tashione asked what time it was. It is 12:30 why? Baby I need two things from you okay. Jazz just looked with a smirk grin on his face waiting for her to ask for the gun. Tashione sat up on the bed and said I need some money and my gun. Jazz did not say anything at first but when he did the only thing that came out was No! Jazz was not trying to hear anything. Tashione begged and pleaded with him but he was not even hearing it. After Jazz took his shower and got dressed, they headed out for Jamaica Ave. to pick up her nameplate. They went to Blimpies to eat and chill for a minute. Tashione asked Jazz why she cannot have the gun back. He told her because it was going to get her in trouble and he did not want that. Jazz grabbed her hand and said come on let us go home. When they got back to his house, nobody was home. Jazz cut on his system playing Tashione favorite songs he had on tape for her. They danced in the room then started kissing and caressing each other. Jazz wanted to take it further but Tashione was not trying to feel it so Jazz looked and said its okay. I can wait and my love is still strong for you. It was getting dark now and Tashione asked Jazz was he hungry? I am a little why? I want some Chinese Food so what do you want to eat. Once she called, the order in Jazz went in his pocket to give her some money. Tashione told Jazz to go ahead and take his shower and have a blunt ready by the time she comes back. Oh, Jazz I got something to give you when I come back and you have wanted this for a long time. Tashione walked up the street to go get the food not worrying about anybody messing with her because she was well known. She got the food then went to the corner store for some cigarettes and beer. Once she was walking back, towards Jazz house out of nowhere, someone grabbed her mouth and Tashione dropped the bags she held. While she was being dragged into a parking lot, she was trying to scream. She tried to fight, bite to get away from the man that had a hold on her. She reached for her gun but it was not there and one of them punched her in the face and she fell down. Tashione was not giving up so quickly. She kept fighting and screaming for help but no one came. The man begins to beat the hell out of Tashione until she was knocked out. As she lay there, motion less one of the men pulled down her shorts and panties then spreading her legs wide. Tashione came through and seen what was about to happen to her and she started to fight again. To no avail, the man forced himself in her and she felt the sharp pain. Tashione had never in her life felt so helpless in her life. After the man was done, he begins to beat Tashione ass until she passed out. They left her there and walked off laughing. Jazz was getting worried because Tashione was not back yet. Jazz put on his clothes and headed for the Chinese Restaurant. He seen food and broken bottle on the ground so he started yelling out Tashione name but no answer. Jazz started looking around and he seen Tashione legs sticking out from between the parked cars. Once he made it to her, he picked her up and started running towards his house. When he got to the door his mother was there looking all shocked and wanting to know what happen. Jazz said I do not know Ma; I just found her in the parking lot like this. Mom-du told Jazz to take her to his room so she can clean some of the blood off her. Tashione still had not came through yet and Jazz called Tashione parents. He let them know what happen and to meet them at the hospital. Jazz covered Tashione in a blanket and held her like she was a child while his mom drove them. Once they got there and the doctor had giving her a full exam; Tashione parents came in the doors. Gene walked straight to Jazz and asked what happen to my daughter? Jazz said she was beat up pretty bad and did not know who did it. The Doctor came out and said Tashione is still unconscious and she was raped. Jazz had started crying, and Rose almost fainted and Gene caught her. Jazz was so mad that he could have killed someone at this moment. Rose grabbed Gene saying; No not my baby! Can I see her now Doctor? Yes you may but do not stay to long; follow me please. They all went in and Tashione looked like a total different person. Rose started crying and went to the bed holding Tashione hand saying its okay Mommy is here now. Gene did not know how to react or show his pain; seeing his daughter lying there like that, so he walked out. Jazz was crying on his mother shoulder saying it was his fault. Mom-du told him; you stop that right now because it was not his fault. Jazz walked over to Tashione saying I am sorry, baby and I hope you can forgive me for letting this happen to you. I promise I will never let anything or anybody ever hurt you again. Tashione I love you please wake up, come on baby wake up for me. Tashione still did not respond to anybody. Jazz voice got a little deeper and louder when he seen that Tashione was trying to open her eyes. Rose ran out to get the Doctor and Tashione opened her eyes looking around her surroundings. Tashione asked where she was and Jazz went to grab her hand and she freaked out saying no do not touch me. Jazz was feelings were hurt but Mom-du went to calm Tashione down. When the Doctor came in the room Tashione was crying and he asked everybody to leave so she could get some rest. Mom-du told Jazz that it was going to take awhile before Tashione would let a man touch her after she was raped and to be patience with her. The Doctor told Rose and Gene that it was going to be hard for her to get over this but they had support group that she could go too. Tashione turned over and started to cry. Jazz went back in the room and Tashione acted liked she was sleep. Jazz pulled a chair up and laid his head on the bed and cried himself to sleep. Tashione started talking in her sleep and that is what woke Jazz up. She was screaming for Jazz to help her. He got on the bed and held her saying I am here baby and it is going to be okay. Tashione begin to settle back down to sleep. Sometime during the night Tashione woke up and seen Jazz sleeping in the chair. She watched him sleep and the tears started to fall again. Jazz heard her crying and woke up he asked her is she okay? Do you want the Doctor? Tashione told him no that she was okay but she was hurting emotionally. Tashione tell me what happen that night? She told him everything and that she did not know who done that to her, she never seen their faces and begin to cry again. Jazz was so mad that he could not hide his true feelings from Tashione. He told her that he was sorry that he could not protect her and please forgive him. I promise you I will never let anything happen to you again. Tashione did not say a word she just looked at him. Tashione stayed in the hospital for a week before they released her. Jazz and Rose was there to pick her up. Jazz tried to help Tashione to the wheelchair but she brushed him off. Jazz felt bad but he also understood that it was going to take time for her to feel safe and comfortable with him again. They made it to the car and Jazz pulled off heading towards her house. Rose asked her did she want something from the store, No ma I just want to go home. Jazz pulled up in the parking lot and when Tashione got out of the car; people started staring at her like she was a freak. Once they made it inside Tashione turned to see the look her mother and Jazz had on their faces and flipped out. Tashione told Jazz she would understand if he did not want her anymore and she ran to her room closing the door. Rose told Jazz that Tashione did not mean anything by that and she's just worried about what other people was thinking of her because of the rape. Jazz said I know but I want to be here for her as well. Jazz told Rose to keep him posted about Tashione and if she needed anything to let him know and then he left.

CHAPTER 3

(present) in the morning Soul was up early cooking breakfast for them. Tashione made her way down to the kitchen and sat on the counter as usual. Soul told Tashione to get her funky ass down and sit at the table so they could eat. Tashione got down and sat in the chair so they could eat. After breakfast, Tashione did the dishes and clean the kitchen back up. Tashione called the Fire Dept to see what information they had about what cause the fire. The chief told her that someone set fire to a bunch of rags under the bed and it was a trail of gasoline to help it spread. He asked Tashione who else has access to her home and she told them her boyfriend Raul does. Tashione hung the phone up and started thinking could Raul actually do something like that to her and why. Then he always acted like that if it was not concerning him so she cancels that thought. Soul asked what did the man said and she lied to her best friend. So what do you want to do today? Tashione said we need to go by Benita's motherhouse and pay our respects. They were dressed and left out. Once we said who we was Benita mother Tracy let us in. They followed her to the living room to where they seen the photo book of pictures of all of them as well as Benita's picture of her growing up. They shared some memories with Ms. Tracy and cried some before it was time to leave. Ms. Tracy had a huge picture of them over her chimney Tashione asked Soul did she remember the day they took that picture. Girl you know I do because Benita kept on talking shit to the man that was taking the picture. Everybody laugh because they knew that Benita was a perfectionist. Once they said their goodbyes, they left and headed back towards Soul house. Tashione was really quiet and so was Soul. Tashione told Soul lets go to the mall for a little bit. Once they got there and was walking toward Tina's Shop Soul stopped dead in her tracks. Tashione looked up and they seen Raul with another woman. Tashione and Soul walked straight up to them to let him know he was busted. Raul was shocked as hell and could not say a word. Tashione told Raul to close his mouth because he was busted.

The woman who was with him asked who is these people? Tashione said I used to be his girl but I guess I was wrong right Raul. Raul said used to be you still are. Tashione said I do not think so! I am not in the business of keeping motherfuckers when they do not want to be kept and walked off. Raul was so mad at himself for being caught he did not even hear the girl say "Fuck you!" and walked off. Tashione got her dress and then they went to White Castles to get something to eat. By the time, they got back to Soul house the telephone was ringing. Soul answered the phone and it was a police officer asking for Tashione. Soul told him to hold on so she could get Tashione. When Tashione got on the phone and said Hello the officer asked her to come to the station to answer some question. I will be there as soon as I can. (Click) Tashione hung the phone up and Soul asked what is up? Tashione told her that she had to go to the police station to be question. Once they got to the station and told the desk clerk who she was the woman officer told her to have a seat. It took about ten minutes for a man to come out of a room to get her. He walked up to her and introduce himself as Detective Greene. After the introductions were made, he asked the women to follow him which they did once inside he asked them to have a seat. Detective Greene started asking Tashione how long did she know Benita? Tashione told him since we were children. He got the same response from Soul but she wanted to know why he was asking them that kind of questions. The Detective asked them about the night of the party. Tashione told him that we were all there from 8:00 p.m. to 2:00 am... After that, I left with my boyfriend Raul to go home. Soul told the Detective that her Benita, Necey stayed to clean up before they went home which we left at 3:15 a.m. and I drop everybody off at home. I do not drink so I was the designated driver that night. I dropped Benita off first because here house was the closest then Necey because she was across town. That was the last time I seen Benita. Tashione asked the Detective how they knew to come to her house. We got your address from Benita's mother and all of her friends. So do you have any reasons why she was killed and is there a suspect yet? Detective Greene said not yet but tells me something did she have any enemies? Tashione and Soul both said No at the same time. He even asked did Benita have an argument with someone at the party. Tashione said no, but Soul said yes she did with Raul but everybody always fall out with him. Why was that the Detective asked. Because Raul and Benita used to date, each other back in High School. Tashione do you think Raul is capable of killing his ex? No Detective, Raul is a lot of things but a killer he is not. Well ladies I want to thank you for coming down and if you can think of anything please give me a call my numbers are on my card. Soul and Tashione left and went by Tashione house to get her some clothes. The house was a mess and Soul was very curious as hell about how the fire got started. Tashione went to her bedroom and started looking around but she never found anything that would help. Tashione came upstairs and just looked at her bedroom. Soul walked up to Tashione and asked her was she okay and hugged her as well. Tashione said yeah I will be okay once I get things in motions. Tashione seen something by the bed that caught her eye, it was a pair of Raul gloves he wore when he rides his motorcycle. Tashione was thinking now and she knew he never brought his gloves in the house. He would always leave them on the stand that they made together. Soul asked Tashione what it is. Oh, nothing girl just found one of Raul gloves that is all. Well let us grab you some clothes out of the closet. When Tashione opened it, all of Raul good clothes were gone. Girl you need to get your locks and security system change ASAP! They started to load clothes up in the trunk and the back seat. They got in the car and headed for Soul house. Once they got back and got all the clothes in the spare bedroom and put up, Soul went to start dinner. The telephone started to ring and it was Necey. Tashione told her to catch a cab to Soul house so they could hang out like before. Necey agreed and hung up. Tashione told Soul that she invited Necey over to hang out. Soul just looked at first and said its okay I will not trip or flip on her. Tashione hugged her and helped cook dinner. By the time, Necey got over to Soul's house dinner was almost ready. Necey just walked on in, and went straight to the kitchen. When she made her appearance known, they all spoke to each other. Necey said let me wash my hands and I will help. They were all sitting at the table eating and drinking wine; and just catching up on the latest. After dinner, they cleaned up and went and sat out back near the pool. Soul was rolling a blunt while Necey and Tashione put their feet in the pool. Soul went in the house cut the radio on and she had speakers set up around the pool. Soul came back out and joined the others and fired up the blunt. While they were smoking, they were talking about all the good ole days they all shared. Tashione even brought up the time when Benita was so high she feel in the pool and we all laughed so much. Soul even remembered the day Benita caught her boyfriend cheating on her saying how she poured her drink in his lap. Still laughing Soul said do you remember when we all went ice skating and Benita fell and broke her wrist and tried to act as if nothing was wrong and the guys that was there was treating her like a baby and Benita loving every minute of it. Tashione got very quiet now just thinking about how she misses her best friend so much. Soul looked at her watch and it was almost 9:00 p.m. she asked Necey does she want them to take her home or do she want to stay over as well. Tashione said yeah chill over here, it will be like a sleep over. Necey said okay and they all walked inside the house Soul cut the radio off and put a tape on which was "How Stella got her Groove Back, while watching TVs'. In addition to getting high the phone rang and Soul answered it saying speak. Once she heard it was Raul she asked Tashione did she want to talk ? Tashione nodded no then Soul hung it up. After a few minutes went by the phone rung again and this time Tashione answered and said Raul, it is over stop calling me then hung up. She picked the phone up and it had a dial tone and left it off the hook so who ever called will get a busy signal. They watched the movie in peace; by the time the movie was finish all three of them was asleep. Tashione somehow woke up and cut the TV off and sat in the love chair and just looked out the window thinking about her past again.(Past) Tashione thought about how her and her friends were chilling in the room listening to the Menudo songs which of course is a Spanish group. Tashione wanted to go outside for a while, She has been stuck in her room since the accident happened to her. They decided to leave and Amise wanted to go as well. You can go but I do not want any trouble out of you. They went to the pizza shop to get some Ices then on their way out Tashione had to see Jazz but in order to do so she had to go pass where she was raped. Amise seen the hesitant in her sister and asked what is wrong? Tashione told her and Amise said it is going to be okay you are not alone. I just know Jazz will be so excited to see you he really do miss you sis. Once

Tashione built her nerves up, they started walking toward his house. Jazz was sitting on the steps when Keith hit Jazz saying oh shit look man. When Jazz turned around and seen Tashione he jumped down and started walking but stop; because he didn't know how to handle her so he wanted her to make the first move. Tashione seen Jazz smiled at her and she took off running towards him. When she reached Jazz, he gave her the biggest hug even turning her around. When he put her down, he looked in her eyes and said he loves her and kissed her right in front of the whole block. Tashione heard someone clearing their throat and she pulled away from Jazz to see his mom smiling at them. Keith told Jazz to come here and when he did, he whispered to him that he had Tiny sitting on the steps watching them. Tashione was watching Jazz and Keith the whole time and seen Tiny stepped down in front of Jazz saying what is up baby? Tashione walked over to them and answered the girl first by saying okay little girl the Queen is back home and you can step off. Jazz would not say anything but just watch his Queen handle her business over her man and the Queen spot. Tiny had a lot of mouth so Tashione punch the girl right in her face. Jazz nodded his head and smiled while Tiny and Tashione got to fighting. Tiny pulled Tashione hair and she flip the fuck out. Tashione was beating Tiny ass so bad that Mom-du told Jazz to break it up right now. When Jazz tried to break it up Tashione pulled out her new gun and pointed it right at the girl's head saying if you ever come back around here again I will kill you! Tashione got up and turned on Jazz cursing him out saying how he been fucking while she was at home dealing with her rape. Jazz said I did not fuck that girl or any other girl Jazz was looking at the gun now. Tashione seen that he was looking at her gun and told him I will never be without it again understand. He wanted to say something but knew it was going to be like this since her raped. He told her she can have her other one back if wanted to. Yeah I will get that from you later but she seen her sister walks over to Ron and started talking. Ron really likes Amise but he was scared of Tashione so he wanted to keep their shit under cover. Keith said let us go to the weed spot and have a smoke session so everybody left but Jazz and Tashione. They went up to his room and Tashione went straight to the radio and cut it on and "Gentle" was playing so she turned it up. Tashione told Jazz come here and dance with me. He wrapped his arms around her and they dance off their song like ole times. Tashione pulled away from him and went to the bed and took her shirt off leaving on her bra and shorts. She asked Jazz to come here and he took off his and got in the bed with her. Jazz crawled on top of Tashione kissing her at first then he pulled her shorts and panties off while she unhooked the bra. She lay there naked and looking very sexy to Jazz, she asked him to make love to her. Are you sure, you want this? Yes, Jazz but you and I both know that I am not a virgin any more and reached for his hand to place them on her titties. Jazz looked Tashione in her eyes and said I have been waiting for this day to come for a long time and my love is still the same as it was when I first told you. Tashione laid back and spread her legs apart and waited for Jazz to come inside of her but what happen next shocked both of them. Tashione started to struggle against him with her eyes close. Jazz told Tashione to open her eyes so she could see it was him and not the rapist. She did as he asked and her body relaxes and he eased in her and made love to her while she watched his every movement. Jazz was real patient with her and once she was really relaxed and got into it, he stroked her a little faster. Tashione felt safe enough to move with him and when she felt her body-getting ready to spasm, she grabbed Jazz shoulders because she was nutting. Jazz got a little rougher and Tashione asked him to stop because it was hurting a little bit. So he slowed down but also told her that when he was about to nut he would get a little fast and rough. Look at me Tashione so you can see that it is me when I come inside of you. She did what he said and it was just like he said it would be and Tashione bite him on the shoulder to help take her mind off the pressure he was causing between her legs and they nut together. Jazz was breathing hard and Tashione loved the after glow of love making with him. When Jazz heart beat calm down he got up used his t-shirt to wipe between her legs and kissed her real tender. He got back in the bed and held Tashione in his arms and then he reached her one of her pacifier so she can fall asleep in peace. A few minutes later Jazz heard Keith calling his name from the window saying come on man. Jazz put on his clothes and told his mom that Tashione was sleeping and he was going downstairs right quick. Keith was rolling the blunt when Jazz made it down. He asked where Tashione was. She is asleep and Ron you need to back up off Tashione lil sister before she comes down and bust a cap in your ass. Keith started laughing and Amise said no she will not because it will hurt me to see her do some shit like that. We will see lil mama! By the time they got half way through Tashione was coming through the doors looking at Ron saying get your hands off my sister ass before you can't grab no more. Come here baby and let your sister be with him as you can see they really like each so chill out. Tashione looked at them and said I got my eyes on you. Look baby I am hungry so go get me something to eat please. Jazz sent Keith and Ron to the Chinese Store to get the food. Tashione got on her little sister about Ron but Jazz told her to stop. Tashione turned around and told him to mind his business; but Jazz walked up to her and grabbed her by the arms. Tashione flipped out and started fighting and screaming at him. Jazz pulled her even closer saying its okay baby; I am here and he just held her while she cried. After a few minutes went by Tashione started laughing instead of crying Jazz said okay what is up now? Tashione said I can deal with the fact that I was raped and we made love today. what I can't figure out is what in the hell gave you the idea that you can move on and start messing with another bitch!! Jazz said I love you and thanks for coming back to me. Tashione told Jazz your not out of trouble yet, so explain! Jazz said she do not mean nothing to me. Tashione asked Jazz did you fuck that girl. Jazz looked at her and dropped his head and said yes. Tashione did not say or do anything until Jazz lift his head and then she punched Jazz right in the mouth and burst his lip. Blood was dripping from his lip and Jazz said okay baby that is enough but Tashione was not even close to being finish. She started cursing Jazz out and then swung again, which caught him in the head. Jazz grabbed Tashione so she could not hit him no more. You bastard why could not you wait until I got better! I knew you would do it eventually and I can't trust you now do you understand me? Doesn't even answer that just let me go okay? Jazz let her go and Tashione told him do it one more time and I will cap you in your ass. Ron and Keith were coming back and they all went up to Jazz bedroom to eat and listen to music. There was a Reggae song that came on and Tashione started dancing and when she started rolling her ass, telling Jazz to come on he got right up grinding on her ass. After everybody ate, they walked

Tashione and Amise home. Right when they got to the building Jazz said I still meant what I said and Tashione just walked away saying goodnight my so call love. Once they got out of sight Jazz and Ron left talking about the two sisters they both were in love with. Instead of the Tashione and Amise going in their apartment they seen their brother get into an argument with some boy and was about to fight. However, when the boy seen Tashione he told her let it is one on one. Tashione knew that many people took him being in a wheelchair that he had no skills but the joke was on the other guy. Even though Tashione loved to fight, she let her brother handle his. Well Divine goes ahead and split that nigga wig or knocks him the fuck out the choice is yours. Divine took it to his ass and left that punk ass lay out on the ground. Tashione, Divine and Amise went in their apartment and their parents seen that Divine lip was busted and asked what happen to his lip? Amise told her daddy that Divine knocks some boy the fuck out! Watch your mouth young lady before I wash it out with soap. Amise told Tashione that she needed to talk to her about Ron so they went into their bedroom closing the door. Tashione lay on her bed and asked Amise what about Ron. I really like him and he like me but you scare him so much and I want you to back off some but if you see him doing something wrong to me then get his ass. Tashione looked at him and said okay but tell him I will be watching him. Amise gave her sister a hug and said thank you. Girl do you know that school is almost here and I know Jazz is giving you some money. Do you think Ron will do the same for me? Let me tell your fast ass something right now he don't got to do shit for you, I got your back but he will do a lil something trust me. Tashione called Jazz and asked him could they all go to the pool in Brownsville in the morning. Yes and I want you here in the morning so don't be late. I promise not to be late and I will wear my two-piece just for you. Oh, hell no wear a one piece or we won't go at all. Jazz okay already damn I want to look good too. Who the fuck are you trying to look good for beside me? Only you baby trust me! I will call you back later on okay. No baby I will see you when you get here in the morning. (Click) Tashione told Amise that she knew Jazz would be with that girl but when she catches him all hell would break loose. She tried calling his house but his mom said he was not there. Therefore, Tashione grabbed her gun and snuck out of her place and headed for Jazz's apartment. When she got almost near the front, she could hear Jazz talking to some female and they are laughing about something. When Tashione heard, Jazz asked the girl for a kiss, that is when she made her presence known and Jazz jumped. When Tashione seen her friend Necey she was hurt and shocked that she wanted to cry but didn't. Tashione looked at Jazz and said that's why you didn't answer my page. You out here trying to fuck with one of my friends behind my back. Jazz stepped up to Tashione and slap her and told her that's right now go home before you get hurt some more. Tashione pulled out her gun and he started running but when Tashione pulled the trigger, the bullet caught him right in his ass and he fell. Necey ran home so she wouldn't have to deal with Tashione. Mom-du came out and they headed for Jazz. Get your ass up boy you know better than to put your hands on her! They took him to the hospital and the Doctor told them they couldn't get the bullet out.

CHAPTER 4

Now they are on their way back home and Tashione helped Mom-du get Jazz back to his room and settled. They were in the bedroom alone now and Tashione asked him why he does it? Jazz couldn't say nothing so Tashione told him from this night on you and me are finished! I'm still the Queen and you will show and give me the respect I'm due and walked out. When Tashione got in the living room Mom-du told her that she heard everything and she wasn't mad and didn't blame her. Tashione left and headed home and nobody ever knew she left the house. After putting on her pajamas, she cried herself to sleep. When she got up in the morning, her mama told her to go to her father's job so he could take her school shopping. Tashione took the bus to Cypress Hills, which would put her in front of his job by the time he got off. When she got off the bus; there was a bunch of girls standing in the way of the building. Tashione was not a punk so she walked toward them. They crowded around her and asked where she was from? Tashione said why and who wants to know? Some girl named Gina said I do and if you don't answer, you will just get your ass kicked until you do. Gina got up in Tashione face and started to talk shit but Tashione pulled her gun out and pointed it at her head. Everybody froze and didn't say a word. Out of nowhere here comes Tashione father asking what is going on? He told Tashione to put her gun down so she did and push the girl away from her. Gina looked at Gene and said you know her? Yes, this is one of my daughters. Gina apologized to Gene and told him you knew how it was down here when strangers come through. Gene asked Gina would she die for these streets that didn't even belong to her. Gina just looked at him before she said this is all I have. Gene told Tashione that he meant to meet her but the bus came early. Tashione started asking questions about Gina and the gang around here. He looked his daughter in the eyes and told her no that is only a portion of that gang. Gene said no Tashione, no more gangs especially not the A-team. Tashione wasn't even listening. They went shopping and got home around 7:30 p.m. and mama was putting dinner on the table. Tashione took her clothes to the room where Amise was at. Girl let me see what all you got. Tell me something is Jazz going to give you the rest of money to get your shoes and the rest of your clothes? We are no longer together since he wants to mess with my friends and I pop his ass. After putting up the clothes and doing the dishes from dinner Tashione wanted to know more about the A-team and be apart of them. The next day Tashione went to her father job around 2:00 to see if she ran into anybody before he got off. Gina and some other girls were walking toward her and spoke. Are you looking for your father? No I was looking for you; my dad said if I wanted some friends around here that you were a good choice. Gina started laughing saying bullshit your father don't like gangs and he is always trying to get me to leave it alone. Okay I want to be apart of your gang satisfied! What will your father think about that? Does he need to know! Gina said okay if you are serious then meet us right here around 7:00 p.m. and be beat in for 10 minutes. If you make it, you are in and if you don't you just got your ass beat for nothing. Tashione went to the corner and caught a cab back home without her father ever knowing she was at his job. When Tashione got home, she asked her mama what time she had to be in the house. You are in the house around 10:00 and I will let your father know I gave you permission. Tashione kissed her mama and said I love you and left. Right when Tashione was almost out the door Rose asked are you packed? Tashione said yes I am. She went on out the door. Tashione got on the bus to go to Cypress Hills once she got there Gina was there with a couple of other girls. They all said what's up then Gina said follow me. They get to the back of the projects and go through an open fence that open up like a garage full of older and younger people. Tashione thought to herself "What the fuck I got myself in to"! A man comes out the back and said so little mama you want to be apart of my family? Yes, I do said Tashione. Listen lil mama I know your father and he's a good man and I don't want no trouble. I know that your father is against gangs fighting, but he is a well respected around here and now his daughter wants to be in the gangs. He asked Tashione does your father know? No he does not are you going to tell him? The leader laughs but says no lil mama I won't tell him. Are you ready lil mama to get beat in? Tashione told him let's do this. Tashione was beat in by five girls her age but she could not swing back but had to remain on her feet. Tashione got in the middle and it started; at first Tashione was straight but when it was almost over Gina tried to trip her up. Tashione was very determine to be apart of this gang so she remained on her feet bleeding from her lip and nose. Once she was beaten in and still standing some of the other girls came over with a towel to clean her up. Then the leader told the family to welcome their new sister. What do you want to be called? Before she could answer, some guy yelled out Brown Eyes. Tashione looked at him and he smiled at her and she said Brown Eyes it is. The leader yells out Welcome Brown Eyes. Everybody started yelling out Brown Eyes and hugging her at the same time.

CHAPTER 5

An hour later everybody was leaving the hide out and Tashione was about to leave; when the guy who gave her the name made his presence known. Tashione asked him so since you gave me my name do I get to know yours? Yes you do and the name is Tony aka Tattoo I'm Gina brother. So tell me why Brown Eyes? Tattoo told her that it was because of her eyes that he gave her the name. It's custom for someone on the guys side to name the female and the same for the girls to name the men in the family. That is so cool said Tashione. Tattoo told her the main rules that she had to hang with her age group, and she could not hang with the older group without permission. Tashione looked at her watch and seen that it was time to go home. Gina told her brother that she would walk her but Tattoo told her to go on home that he would walk her to the bus stop and make sure that she gets on. Tattoo asked Brown Eyes did she have a boyfriend. No I don't! He asked her how old she was next. I am 14 yrs old and why all the questions? I want to know that's all and I'm 17. The conversation was going really well till Tattoo wanted to kiss. Tashione told him don't and Tattoo asked why not? Tashione didn't answer at first but after awhile she told him that she didn't know him and he didn't know her. Well let's get to know each other now and then we will see. The bus came and Tashione got on and wave mouthing the words goodbye. Once Tashione made it home, Jazz was in front of her building waiting. Tashione walked straight to him and asked what it is now Jazz. He told her that she was needed and reached her the gun that he took from her. Well let's go slow ass! Who got hurt Jazz? Jazz told her that Keith was in the hospital from a gunshot wound and he already in the recovery; and should make it but Ron and your sister was with him. Tashione got scared and asked where my sister is now? Amise is with mom-du and she is okay. They all got together in front of Jazz building and talked about how they were going to handle this. Everybody wanted revenge, someone was going to pay with blood or death. Tashione asked Ron who shot Keith? He said Jerome and his posse did this! Tashione took over telling everybody to load up and have your shit because I want blood. All you could here was guns being loaded and people getting in cars. Once they all got to Brownsville and parked the cars a good distance from where they had to go.They seen Jerome and his Posse sitting in the middle of the building waiting. Everybody was so tense at first because they didn't know what to expect from Tashione. All they really knew was that they had to defend the LAC Posse territory and get revenge for Keith being shot it was their code of honor. Jazz said okay let's go and handle this. Once the LAC Posse got into view of Jerome, Jazz said what's up Rome! Rome started laughing while he got up and then said fuck this and swung out at Jazz. Jazz was ready and everybody let them fight one on one. Rome almost had Jazz till he fuck around and let it slip that he was the one that rape his Queen!! Tashione heard what he said and pulled her gun out and called Rome name and when he turned around, she shot him in his chest till there were no more bullets left in the clip. She was about to reload the gun when Jazz grabbed her saying that's enough baby he's dead now it's over. All of Rome Posse was screaming and running and some even fell to the ground for cover. Tashione wanted all of them dead but Jazz didn't let her finish the job. His voice sounded so far away but he managed to get her in the car. When they got back to Jazz place, Tashione was quiet and it scared Jazz a lot because she was never that way and he didn't like it at all. Tashione told Jazz that she was leaving to go home and told Amise to come on. Jazz said okay and for Ron to walk them home. When they made it out the door Jazz called Tashione mother and told her what happen and Tashione should be home soon and hung the phone up. Once Ron seen that they made it okay he turned around and went home. Tashione went straight to her stepmother and told her what happen without Rose even mentioning that she knew what happen. Rose told Tashione it will be okay and she will handle it. The next day the police was at Tashione door. When she open the door and called out Ma the police is here Rose came out of the kitchen and said may I help you. The police officer said is your daughter Tashione home so we could ask her a few questions. Rose opened the door and told them to come on in and have a seat in the living room. They all sat at the table and Rose told Tashione to come out here. When she came out, she sat right next to her mama. One officer asked Tashione was she a member of the LAC Posse? Tashione looked the man in the eyes and said no. The other cop asked where she was at last night around 11:00p.m... Tashione told him I was in my bedroom why? The officer told them that a young man was shot and killed in his projects. Rose asked him what that got to do with my daughter she is never out passed 9:00 p.m. and is not a part of any gangs. All my children have curfews and they have to be in by 9:00 every night unless they are with me and her father or older relatives. The officer said thank you and if your daughter hears something about the shooting please give us a call. Rose walked them to the door and when she close it she turned around and told Tashione she got to lay low and follow her direction cause the cop is going to be watching her now. The next couple of days Tashione followed all the rules and her daddy knew something was wrong because Tashione never followed the rules. He asked Rose what is going on with Tashione? I bet she is in some kind of trouble and you are covering it up for her. No Gene, I'm not covering anything up for her she is scared about something. And it has to do with her rape and I told her that she have to be in at a certain time to avoid anything like this ever happening to her again. Gene knew she was lying to him but let the whole matter go. Several weeks have passed and nothing happened but the cops were still watching the LAC Posse. Tashione called Jazz and asked him to meet her at the pizza shop to get a letter from her. When she goes to meet Jazz and the police are watching the whole time and Tashione does not even notice it but Jazz does. Jazz told Tashione to get rid of the letter that the police are watching him. They act like they don't even know each other and Jazz leaves with an ice cream. When Tashione leave, she has a slice of pizza and soda in her hand when she notices that the police had him up against the car and handcuff him. She leaves and goes to mom-du house and told her that they just picked Jazz up. Mom-du told Tashione to go home and she will go get Jazz and have him to call her later. She tear up the letter and then bounce her ass on home to wait for the phone call. Tashione was getting scared and nervous about Jazz and decided to leave; but before she left she seen Jazz coming in her building looking real upset. Hey, what's wrong with you? How about they talking bout they got my fingerprints on the bullets that was used in a murder. Now we both know that you was the one that shot Rome and they are trying to frame me. Listen I don't want you to come around the way till this shit is over and you still got your

Queen spot unless someone want to fight you for it and you lose and he left without saying another word to her. Mom-du was always down with her children and Tashione because she was apart of the family as well. Tashione went in her house and called mom-du and told her what Jazz just said and mom-du told her to just lay low for a while and don't call that she will call her. Tashione decided to go chill with her new family A-Team. When Tashione get to the hide out and give her name, she was allowed to enter the place. Tattoo was there as well and he said where have you been lately? Right when she was about to answer Tattoo said we already know about you killing Rome. We don't blame you for that but what we don't like is that you didn't let us know. Brown Eyes told him that her mother told her to lay low and don't say a word that is why I did not say anything bout it okay. I just got to let things cool off so since I was tired of being in the house I came here is that cool or am I out! Tattoo told her no wonder you acted so strange when I tried to kiss you. I don't blame you at all and no you is not out but the leader wants to talk to you. So what is the deal with Jazz? Brown Eyes told him that she is the Queen of LAC Posse but I am not with Jazz anymore; but he still have to give me my respect as the Queen. I got raped because I was the Queen and he decide to fuck around while I'm trying to deal with it and I catch him with one of my friends and I pop his ass. Tattoo starts to laugh saying yeah right in the ass! So Brown Eyes what's up with you and me kicking it? Since when is it a, you and me! I'm going to have you and you know you want me so tell the truth. See what you fail to realize is that I can protect you with the A-Team and I can provide for you as well. Brown Eyes was listening and Tattoo said if you wear my chain, people will know not to fuck with you period. Brown Eyes let Tattoo put his chain around her neck and sealed it with a kiss. Brown Eyes turned around and said you are a very brave man to kiss a female who has a gun pointed at his balls. Tattoo said well I always go after what I want and I want you Tashione. Tattoo wanted to know when her birthday was and she told him since you can find out everything else bout me find that out. Oh, trust me baby I will, but just tell me to keep from going through all the trouble. Okay my birthday is June 14 and yours is what June 7, see I know more about you than you know bout me. Well listen my family is having me a party this Saturday and I want you there and you can meet the rest of my family. Are you hungry because I am? They went to White Castle to get a couple of shit burgers, which everybody called them now. After they ate and goes, back to the hide out to chill and talk; Tashione notice that it is getting late and she got to be getting home. Come on I will take you home in my car so you will be safe. When they get there Tashione is about to get out when Tattoo said wait here and gave her a kiss and touched the chain with his name on it. When he got in the car, he told her to tell Jazz doesn't fuck with the property or he's a dead man. Tashione said okay and walked toward her building and to her apartment. Divine said whose chain you have on? Gene looked and said oh you joined the A-Team anyway. Is that Tattoo chain you got on too? Tashione I'm tired of telling you to stay out of trouble so I decided to put you in a girls group home till you get your act straight. Tashione looked at her stepmother and said I won't go and you can't make me. Gene said that's why you are going first thing in the morning now go to your room now and get your stuff packed. Tashione goes but she called Tattoo and told him what was getting ready to go down. Tattoo told her to hold on so he could ask his mom can she stay there. When he comes back on the phone, he told her to get her clothes together and he was on his way. Tashione got as much as she could and waited till her parents went in their bedroom before she left out. Tashione put the letter to her parents on the fridge and eased out to Tattoo car. He told her that he would take her shopping in the morning before the party. My mom said you can stay but you must sleep with Gina and Licet. When they got to his house, his mother was there with the door open and took the bags and hugged her. Welcome to my home Tashione and you know to sleep with Gina right. Now I want you to go get some sleep because we got a big day in the morning.

CHAPTER 6

(PRESENT) When Tashione woke up she heard Soul and Necey arguing over who was going to cook. Tashione started laughing and said look I will cook just get your asses to the table. When they sat down Tashione grabbed three bowls and spoons sat it down then got the milk and cereal and said eat up kiddos. Everybody just laughed and Soul said you were dead wrong for that shit. Soul asked Necey was she riding with them to the funeral and she said yes. Tell me what time to be here. You be here around oh hell no we will pick your ass up so we won't be late so be ready at 1:30 and we can follow the family car. Necey said okay I will be ready. After everybody clean up and took their showers and got dress Soul took Necey home and they went to the grocery store. Soul ran into Raul and she acted as if she didn't see him, but Raul was calling her name all loud so she turned around and asked him what the fuck he wants? Raul started laughing and said how is Tashione doing and holding up since her friend passed? Soul told Raul that Tashione is doing very good since she dumped his ass. That statement pissed Raul off so much that he had to walk off before he ended up kicking her ass. Soul just laughed at him before she left to go to the car. When she gets in her car and leave, she notices that Raul is following her. Right when she gets ready to go another route, he kept going. Soul was really tripping out now and had to get herself together. When she pulled up in the driveway Tashione came out running towards her saying where the hell have you been? It doesn't take this long to drop Neccy ass at home!! Chill out girl I went to the grocery store as well and ran into Raul as well. Tashione calmed down and help her carry the bags in the house. Girl what is going on with you lately? Tashione just walked away and Soul was on her ass once Soul caught up with her, she grabbed her arm to stop her. Tashione turned around and said I don't know what it is but I know something is wrong. I keep thinking about my child hood and all the shit I went through and how I met everybody including my gangs' members who I haven't thought about in a long time. Well girl maybe it's time to call them up just to check in. Maybe it's a sign you just haven't put the clues together yet. Soul gave Tashione a hug and said give it time. Soul cut the radio on and it's playing one of Luther songs and Tashione grabbed a beer and sat down humming the song. They heard a car pull up and when Tashione looked out it was Raul pulling up playing their song. She turns around and told Soul can you believe this fool has come over here and for what. Raul didn't get out of the car either and Tashione never goes out to see what he wants either. Since nobody made an effort to come to the door, he started blowing the horn. Tashione came out and he stop. Raul looked at her and said you look so good. Baby I'm sorry for everything I have done to you, and will you please forgive me and give me another chance? Have you lost your fucking mind Raul or are you on some kind of drugs; because I will never take you back so being gone. Raul looked at her with the most evil eyes she ever seen, but she didn't care because it was over between them. Tashione asked Raul what you want from me now. Raul smiled, and then said you!!! Tashione said you drove all this way to tell me you want me back? That's bullshit Raul please try again. He cut the car off and let the radio play and one of Tashione songs came on called "Love me" by Faith and she dropped her head with tears in her eyes. She was thinking bout all the times they had made love off that song, but she snapped back real quick. Tashione told him to leave and never to come back that it was over for good. Raul wasn't trying to hear any of that shit so he kept on begging her to give him another chance. Look Raul there is nothing between us any more and I don't want to ever see you again. Raul grabbed Tashione and she freaked out slinging her arms and screaming. Raul didn't know what to do then, so he started to hold her down so she couldn't hit him any more. Out of nowhere, Soul came up and started fighting him he let Tashione go and got kicked in his nuts. Raul went down and Soul and Tashione go back in the house telling Raul to leave before they call the police. Once in the house they both calmed down and rolled a blunt. Tashione looked out the window and seen that Raul was gone. Hey, how about I cook dinner and you take a nice hot bath and dinner will be waiting on you Tashione. I think that would be a good idea and maybe it would help me to relax as well. She went up the stairs and got her some clothes to put on and ran some bath water with some vanilla beads in it. When the tub was full, she got in and leaned back and closed her eyes. While relaxing she started to drift off and went back to the past. (Past) Tashione was at Tattoo house just relaxing one afternoon with Tattoo mom. They have really gotten close since she has been staying there. And Tattoo has been staying home more often since Tashione has been there. Tashione asked Cinnamon where was Tattoo's father at and she said he's around and that he comes by every so often. Tony is my oldest and he considers himself the man of the house. I let him pretty much, run the house, and pay the bills. Tashione heard someone called her nickname out "Brown Eyes" she went to the window and it was Tony with some Chinese food saying come help me baby. Tashione took off to go help and forgot to put some shoes on her feet. Cinnamon yelled for her to put shoes on her feet but Tashione was already gone. When she got downstairs, Tony was happy to see her and gave her a kiss. When he pulled back he notice that she didn't have on no shoes on and he flipped, telling her to get on his back so they can go upstairs. Tashione got on his back and they took the elevator to the apartment. Tashione knew that he was mad so she grabbed the food and head for the kitchen with Tony right behind her. What the hell is wrong with you coming down the stairs with no shoes on? Tashione didn't answer him at first; but she put her hand on her hip, then told him I forgot I was just happy to see you. How can I ever forget! shit I got so many pairs of shoes I can open my own shoe store. Tony slapped Tashione and said you little ungrateful bitch! I take care of you and you will talk to me with respect. Tashione was crying but she wasn't going to back down and Cinnamon knew this so she got involved by telling Tony that was enough. Tony gave his mother a look she has never seen before and she even shut up. Tony told Tashione to go to the bedroom and wait for him. Tashione said fuck you I'm not your fucking child but your girlfriend. Tony went to grab her but she ran in the bedroom locking the door. He was banging on the door telling her to open the fucking door. Tony just leave me alone you don't love me like you say, you just want someone to own and I'm not having it okay. The next knock was Cinnamon asking her to open the door, when she did Cinnamon came in and said he is gone. Tashione went to lie on the bed and Cinnamon pulled her hair from her face and said he means well; but he just too over protective of the ones he loves. Tashione told Cinnamon that she was tired of being hurt by him and she was going to leave him if he doesn't stop. Cinnamon I believe Tony is cheating on me and if I catch him and his puta I 'm going cap both their asses. Tony was waiting for the rest of the family to come in so they could eat dinner like a family. Everybody knew something was wrong because nobody was talking. Tony said grace and started fixing his plate then passing the food around. After dinner was done and the kitchen was cleaned back up, Gina asked Tashione to come with her to the hide out for a little bit. Tony said no but Tashione wasn't even trying to hear shit. Tony knew why he didn't want Tashione there and he wasn't ready to hear the bullshit that was to follow behind it so he didn't say shit. Gina and Tashione left and when they got to the hide out everybody was saying what's up Brown Eyes! Where have you been? Yo, Tattoo has been keeping me on lock down but not no more, so what has been going on here? There was a girl named Puddin there and she said she was Tattoo new girl. Gina where is your brother at any way he was suppose to meet me here. Tashione looked at Gina saying you knew all this time and you didn't say a word to me, how could you! Tashione just listen to me I didn't know anything about them I swear it please believe me. Puddin was popping shit and Tashione moved Gina out of the way and said I don't think so; the only thing you can be is a play toy bitch! Puddin and Tashione got to beefing then Tashione punched Puddin in the face. Then all hell broke loose Tashione was stomping the shit out of Puddin when they got Tashione off Puddin she was a shitty mess. Puddin pulled a razor out and cut Tashione right hand. Yo, Gina I'm cut girl! Gina told her to hold it so the skin wouldn't roll back! Puddin told Brown Eyes to tell Tattoo she needed to talk to him. Gina had gotten some cloth and tied it around the cut. Brown Eyes grabbed Puddin ass again and finish beaten that ass. Puddin was begging for her to stop, but the kicks kept on coming till Gina told Tashione to stop. Tashione told Gina she was out and didn't want to talk to her right now. Puddin walked out of there holding her stomach while she was bleeding from every place you could see. Brown Eyes caught a cab to the apartment and when she got there Tony was smoking a blunt with his friends. The guys spoke and Tony said you back early. Tashione raised her hand and said yeah I guess I am. Tony saw the blood stain on the cloth and jumped up picking Tashione up and carrying her upstairs. What happen to you baby? Are you okay? When they made it in Tony yelled out ma come quick Tashione is cut and bleeding. Cinnamon came out with towels and cleaning medicine. After her hand was cleaned up and bandage up she asked Tony why he didn't want her to go to the hide out? Tony tried to explain but Tashione slapped him. Tony saw his mother standing in her doorway shaking her head at him. Tashione started crying and Tony told her it was a mistake and it will never happen again. Tashione got up and showed him her hand saying this is what you play toy did to me. Tashione went to their bedroom and pulled out her suitcase saying she was leaving him. Tony grabbed the suitcase begging and pleading with her not to leave and give him another chance. Tashione let the suitcase go and told Tony to leave her alone. Tashione went to the living room and looked out

The window crying. Cinnamon came out and hugged Tashione saying it's going to be okay baby. Tony was in the bedroom throwing shit around when the telephone rung. Tashione picked up the phone to hear Tony saying bitch don't call my house no more and hung up! Cinnamon told Tashione she knew that she was in love with her son and they will get through this. Tony called out for Tashione to come to the bedroom and when she got in there; she looked him dead in his eyes and said what in the hell do you want from me now! Is it not enough that you broke my fucking heart? I actually thought you loved me, shit I been living in your mother house with you for all these months and everything you said to me was a lie. You get pussy on the regular bases so why cheat on me? Can you answer that for me? Tony told Tashione that he just fucked her and she doesn't mean shit to me. That's why I stop going to the hide out because I did not want to see her. I was drunk and high and she said she wanted to suck my dick, then I fucked her in front of the guys. I love you and only you please believe me when I say this to you. Look Tony I will forgive you but it will take some time for me to get over this shit okay. The phone rung and Tony answered it and he was really quiet that Tashione couldn't hear shit except what!!! Tony hung the phone up and turned to Tashione and said Puddin is in the hospital. Good for that bitch I bet she won't fuck with me any more. She had a miscarriage baby! Oh I'm suppose to feel sorry for her is that what you thought was going to happen. Well let me tell your ass this if you go near her I will leave your ass for good. Tony was a little hurt because he always wanted kids and Tashione wanted to wait.

When pudding got out of the hospital, she made Tony life a living hell by always calling him and asking him to come see her. Which of course he didn't because Tashione would leave him and he didn't want that to happen. One night Puddin went to the hide out to see if Tony would be there and he was so Puddin step up to him and wanted to talk. Tony was a little pissed off, he didn't want to be bothered with her. Puddin wanted another baby by him and she promise to stay away from Tashione. Tony knew she was full of shit so he didn't fuck with her at all. All this shit was taking its toll on Tashione and Tony relationship they even had the phone number changed and Tony beeper number too. Things had gotten better after that and Tashione felt a whole a lot better. School was coming up and Cinnamon took the younger ones to get clothes and Tony took all the older ones to Jamaica Avenue. Tashione went to her favorite store where the sales lady knew Tashione style by hard. She asked Tashione what she can get her today. Tashione told the lady to bring out the racks that they haven't put out yet. I want the hottest shit that nobody got yet. Tony looked at Tashione and told her not to hot okay you belong to me. The sales lady led Tashione to the rack of clothes that had all colors of ¾ quarter length skirts, so when she seen the cream and green outfit she had to have it. Licet even got one to and by the time they were done, Tony was almost broke and they didn't even have their shoes yet. Tony told Tashione that he wasn't going to spend a lot of money on shoes this time and to get two pairs only. Once they got in the first shoe store Licet got her a pair of Fila's sneaker and a pair of shoes. Tashione asked Tony for one hundred dollars and let her do her thing. When she came out, she had a pair of Fila's sneaker and five pair of shoes as well. Tony looked and told her you are not slick. I don't know how you did it but come on I'm hungry now. Licet wanted McDonalds as usual and Tashione told her she was going to turn into a Big Mac one day. After they got their food, Jazz was coming in the door with some of the other members. Tashione tried to act as if she didn't see him but Tony notice them too. Jazz walked over to Tashione saying what's up girl! Tashione said what's up Jazz. I see you looking good Keith and Ron. Jazz told Tashione that she doesn't come around anymore and I was thinking that you were forgetting your role with the LAC Posse

CHAPTER 7

Tony was getting mad as hell because Tashione told Jazz she would be there tomorrow. Jazz spoke to Tony but he never spoke back and told Brown Eyes to come on. Tony told Tashione she would not be going any where near Jazz and when she tried to say something he cut her off. Tashione waited for him to cool down before she even brought it back up. After they ate, they were going to the bus stop to wait for the bus. Tashione told Tony that she was still the Queen of the LAC Posse and he knew this before they got together. Tony you don't have to worry about Jazz; it has been over for a long time now and I love you and only you. The bus pulled up and they got on Tashione was getting really pissed off because Tony would not say anything to her. She grabbed Tony's chin to make him looked at her but he started speaking Spanish real fast. Tashione said you know I can't understand you so speak English to me. Tony grabbed Tashione's hand and squeezed it to get her attention. When she looked into his eyes he told her; it's a shame that you won't even take the time to learn your father language. And the sad part about it is you is half Spanish yourself. If you want to talk to me do it in Spanish or don't talk to me at all!! Okay you want me to talk to you in Spanish here's you're Spanish and started cussing him out in Spanish. Tony said it's a start and started laughing. Tony told Licet when she talks to Tashione do it in Spanish only. Licet thought it was real cool to teach Tashione her other language. Tony and Licet were talking Spanish just to get on Tashione nerves and it was working. She was so mad that when the bus stop she got off and left them with all the bags. By the time she made it to the apartment Cinnamon seen that she came in by herself. Tony and Licet were knocking on the door and Cinnamon went to open the door. Tony called out Tashione name and told his mother that he was going to make Tashione learn Spanish. Tony you can't make her learn Spanish. Oh but I can mama and she will if she want to talk to me. Tashione was so determine not to learn and she had her own weapon to use against Tony ass. Cinnamon told Tashione to come sit next to her. Baby why you don't want to learn how to speak Spanish? I just don't care for it, my father was making me learn against my will, and when I did not speak it right, he fussed so I gave up. Tony jumped in the conversation and he was talking Spanish and told Tashione that he will help her and not fuss. He got up and grabbed her bags and went to the bedroom to put her clothes up. Tony was looking at all the clothes and shoes she had and just shakes his head. Tony had talked to his mom about them sharing a room , at first she wasn't hearing it but later agreed. Tashione heard Tony calling her name and went to his bedroom saying okay baby I will learn how to speak Spanish. Tony smiled and said that's great but that's not why I called you in here. Tony pulled her in his arms and said close your eyes, he turned her around and told her she can open them. Tashione started screaming saying oh baby this is so good. Tashione took off to find Cinnamon and gave her a hug saying she loved her so much. Tony called Tashione back in the room and he told her she had to find some room to put all her stuff up. Tashione told Tony that she won't go shopping no more I'm so happy now. We don't have to sneak around to make love any more. Yes and I can wake up to your jazzy ass mouth and hear you sneaking to suck on that pacifier you call yourself hiding from me. Tashione seen all their pictures on the dresser and jumped right on the bed. Oh, no mama said no sex till everybody goes to bed. That is no fun baby but I can handle it if you can especially when I am naked. Tony got on his knees in front of Tashione and asked her to marry him? Tashione looked in his eyes and said yes baby I will be your wife. Cinnamon started screaming and Tony and Tashione came out running out the room. When Tony seen his little sister all bloody and her eyes were shut he flip out. Cinnamon said Tashione help me get some rags and towels together so we can help stop the bleeding. Gina its going to be okay we are taking you the hospital. Tony picked his sister up and said it's going to be okay I'm here now. Cinnamon told Licet to stay with the younger ones till we get back. Once they got to the hospital they ran all kind of test and the only thing that was wrong was some broken ribs and her left arm was broke in two places. They released her several hours later with some medicine for the pain. They got to the apartment and Cinnamon told Tony to put Gina in her bedroom so she could rest more comfortable. Tony asked her who did this to you. Gina looked at the door and seen Tashione standing there and didn't want to say anything. Tony asked her again and she responded by saying Puddin and her friends beat me with a bat. Tashione looked Gina in her eyes and said I got this one don't worry bout it. Gina told Tashione that she did not want her to get into any more trouble since the last time she got in trouble. Gina started crying and Tashione told her I promise I won't do any thing stupid. Cinnamon came in the room and told everybody to get out so she could rest. Tashione and Tony went to their bedroom to change clothes; when they came out, they both had on all black and strapped. Tony's beeper was going off and it was the A-Team code. They got to the hide out and were filled in on all the shit that took place. They found out that Shorty was cut in her face and arms and was still at the hospital. Tashione told all the other girls that Puddin was hers and she wants her now! No Waiting or Delays! Tashione walked up to Tony and kissed him and said where can we find her baby? He told her he will show her just in case some men are there. They all got in the A-Team van headed for Puddin hang out spot. Pulling up a block away and Tashione was the first one to get out seeing if she could see Puddin. Puddin was on the corner with some friends smoking a blunt when the A-Team trapped them off. When Puddin seen that Tashione had them blocked off she drop the blunt. Tashione said what's up now Puddin! Puddin went to run but Tashione grabbed hold of her hair to keep her from getting away. Tashione said I want your home girls to see you get your ass beat A-Team style. That's when the rest of them came out and just beat the hell out of Puddin and her friends. Puddin was quiet now but she knew the deal with Tashione and all the shit she heard was true. Let's wrap this shit up so I can handle this bitch! Tashione seen that Puddin girls were being laid out so she started beating Puddin ass. Puddin was trying to fight back, but Tashione had her. Puddin manage to get loose and pulled out a razor and swung the shit from side to side. Tashione told her to put the razor down and fight straight up. Puddin was no fool so she kept on swinging the razor, so Tashione pulled out her gun and shot Puddin in her right leg. Tashione told China to bring her a bat and then told Tony to watch his play toy get knock the fuck out. China held Puddin up and Tashione swung the bat; it landed across the chest. Puddin screamed out for help but no one was there to help her. Tashione told her you like bats right, well I want you to meet mines and hit the girl in the head knocking her ass out cold. I want them all laid out A-Team style. Tony walked up to Tashione and said that's enough! Tashione told him don't ever tell me when I had enough. If you hit one more, I will beat your ass myself and I mean it so stop the bullshit. Tashione looked at Tony and said she must mean a lot to you for you to go up against me? No Tashione she doesn't but I'm ready to go and we got her back for my sister. She threw the bat at Tony and pulled her gun on him. Tony just stood there at first, then he told Tashione that he loved her not Puddin. Tashione put the gun down and walked to his open arms. Everybody was heading for the van then Tony pulled off. Once they got back to the hide out Tony still wouldn't say shit to Tashione. They finally made it home and Tony waited till they were in the bedroom before he cursed her ass out. Tashione didn't back down she got right up in his face as well. Tony slapped the shit out of Tashione and she went crazy fighting him back. Tony grabbed her by the neck chocking her. Tashione felt herself giving out, but she managed to pull her gun out and pointed it to his head. Tony hurried up and let go and begged her not to shoot him. Tashione looked at him and told him you aren't even worth the bullet and drop the gun on his bed. Tashione opened the door slammed it shut and went for the front door. Tony was looking out the window and seen her walking up the street so he started calling her name out; but Tashione would not respond to him. Tashione walked all the way to Jazz place and Mom-du looked at her and held out her arms to her. Tashione went and started crying at the same time asking why she can't live a normal life? Mom-du told her she got to fight to survive in the streets of New York and you know this. Tashione pulled back wiping her face saying I know this but I'm tired. Jazz came in the door and seen a hand print on her face and marks around her neck. Who did this to you Tashione? It really don't even matter Jazz so stop stressing it okay I'm alright. Jazz pulled Tashione up and lead her to his bedroom closing the door. Tashione got on his bed and laid down telling Jazz that she won't make it much longer if she stayed in New York. Jazz asked her what you have done now. She sat up and said do I have to tell you even though you know my specialty. Jazz why am I so quick to shoot people and why do I have this obsession with guns? Jazz could not answer her question but he could hold her for support. He finally told her that he thinks it because of her being hurt so many times and the guns make her feel safe. Tashione fell asleep in his arms and he laid her down and went to talk to his mother about Tashione. They decided to call Tashione parents and let them know that Tashione was at their house and was okay. Tashione father said thank you I will be there in a few minutes to pick her up and hung up the phone. Tashione heard the conversation and before Jazz and mom-du knew it, she was gone but she left a note for them and her parents. In the note to Jazz, she asked him to keep her gun but she will be back for it. Tashione started walking back toward Tony house and she seen him sitting on the front steps with his head down. Tashione told him we need to talk and he picked her up saying he loved her and that he was sorry. Tony told Tashione that they could talk later but he wanted to make love to her. They did just that make love all through the night. The next morning when she woke up Tony little sister Tam was in the bed with her. She went to move but Tam was all under her. Tashione eased out of bed and went to the bathroom to wash her face and brush her teeth. Cinnamon was sitting at the table drinking coffee. Morning ma and sat down across her and Cinnamon told her you got to slow down baby before you end up dead. Tony told me what happen and I agree with him. I know this and I need to get away from this life but I don't want to leave Tony. Cinnamon said I want you to think about this real hard and when you make up your mind, I will help you any way I can okay baby. Tashione said okay and asked where Tony was at this early in the morning? I sent him to the store for some things I need to cook later on. Tony was just walking in the door hands full of bags and a smile on his face. Tony put the bags down and gave Tashione a kiss and told her good morning. How did Tam end up in the bed with me? She had to get in the bed when I left to go to the store for mama. Tashione got her some bread and toasted it while Cinnamon was making breakfast. Everybody was getting up when they smelled food. After breakfast was done, they started taking baths and putting on clothes. Tashione asked Gina how she was feeling. I feel much better but you promise me you would stay out of trouble. You don't think you went to far this time? No baby I don't so stop worrying yourself about it okay everything will be just fine. Tashione I want you to give up the gang and make me a titi (auntie)! Tashione told Gina she would think about it but deep down she was ready to give it up. She went in the bedroom and Tony was putting lotion on his body and Tashione just stared thinking what it would be like to have his children. Tashione called Tony name and when he looked up, she told him that she was ready to give up the gang and start a family. He thought she was pregnant now but she told him that she was not certain. Tony was so excited yelling "Yes baby" Cinnamon came in and asked what is all the noise for? Ma how about she might be having a baby! Oh, Tashione that is good news but first goes to the doctor and sees. No ma I'm going to get a test now! After Tashione took, the test it showed up positive and everybody was so happy. School was starting that Monday and Tashione was going through the morning sickness, which she hated. Tashione could not stand the smell of food being cooked, so she went outside till Cinnamon was done. Well it's time for school and Gina, Licet and Tashione was all dressed and waiting on Tony slow ass. They all walked Tam and Licet to their school and then they headed for Thomas Jefferson School. Once they got there on school grounds, they seen some of the other members and they all spoke and the guys smoked a blunt before going in the school. The first bell was going off and Tony walked Tashione to her homeroom and told her he will try to meet up with her afterwards to walk her to the next class. It was now lunch time and Tashione was feeling sick from the smell of food. Tony told Tashione to come on so he could get her out of there and get her something to eat as well. Tashione ate her lunch and then reached for Tony sandwich as well. Damn girl you eat too much; I can't even eat around you any more. Oh fuck you Tony; you wouldn't be saying that if I wasn't pregnant either. Oh come here baby I was only playing with you and he gave her a kiss. It was time to get back to school and when they got to the doors of the cafeteria they seen that Charlie was acting a fool since he was high. He was trying to crack on some girl and she didn't want to be bothered by him. Charlie set the garbage can on fire and dumped the shit on the girl. She was screaming and the guards came in running to help the girl. Tashione started throwing up her lunch and Tony lead her out. Tony walked Tashione to her class telling her he will see her when school was letting out and to meet him by the stairs. When the last bell rung Tashione went to meet Tony and was trying to get to him, but someone started pushing and Tashione felled down the stairs. Tony seen the whole thing and could not do anything to help her. When Tony made it to her, he helped her up and they started walking home. Tashione felt blood running down her legs and told Tony. He picked her up and ran home so his mother could help him out. Cinnamon was looking out the window and seen Tony carrying Tashione, she knew something was wrong so she came down the stairs. Cinnamon flagged a cab down and they went to the hospital. After waiting several hours, the Doctor came out and told them that Tashione had lost the baby and Tony yelled NO! Tony asked could he see her and when he opens the door Tashione was in bed crying. Tony went to hold her and said we will have another baby it will be okay. They both held on to each other and cried for the baby they just lost.

CHAPTER 8

(Present) Tashione jumped up and Soul was there standing in the door way saying okay sleepy head dinner is ready. I will be down as soon as I get some clothes on, Soul pulled the door close and Tashione got out and got dress. They ate dinner in the living room so they could watch a movie called "Belly." The phone rung and Soul was saying no, no she do not want to talk to you and hung up. Tashione looked at Soul and said thanks a lot. Tashione finish eating and grabbed Soul's plate to wash the dishes. She told Soul that she was going to go to bed early; all right girl I will see you in the morning. Soul picked up the phone and dialed Necey number, when Necey answered Soul said what is up? Necey said nothing much this way! How is Tashione holding up? Soul told her she could be better if Raul would just leave her alone. I hear you girl, but we could all just beat the shit out of him and just leave his ass there. Soul started laughing and said we will be there at your house at 1:00 so please be ready. I will but just call me to make sure I am awake okay. (Click) The next morning Soul called Necey to see if she was up getting ready and she was; but Necey asked her to pick her up a pair of panty hose in black. All right but be ready when we get there I mean it Necey or you is a left ass. Tashione got up and took a quick shower and put on her clothes and went down the stairs to get a cup of coffee and seen Soul sitting at the table. Good morning girl, how did you sleep? Okay I guess but I am just thinking about Benita and how could something like this happen to sweetest person in the world. Tashione went and hugged Soul saying I know just what you mean and I miss her too. Did you call Necey to see if she was up? Yes and she want me to pick her up a pair of black stockings on our way. Do you want some breakfast? No I am not hungry yet but we could grabbed something later and bring extra cash for our broke ass friend Necey. Soul laughed, saying you are so crazy but telling the truth you are. They got in the car and headed for Necey house; Soul got the stockings from the gas station and the several minutes later pulling up in Necey driveway blowing the horn. Necey came out saying please tell me you got that for me? Yes, girls get your ass in the car and put them on in the car. Necey was putting the stocking on and Tashione said do you'll remember when we was all going out and Benita was trying to put stockings on in the car. Soul said yeah I do remember and she fucked up three pairs before we even got to the club they all just laughed. They finally reach Benita mother house; and went inside and seen all the family member and Benita two sisters who looked just like her. Things still did not ring right about Benita death and she made a promise she would keep on the police so they could find out who killed her. They were loading up in the family cars and their own cars. When they arrived at the church, the family was being led to their seats. Tashione, Soul, and Necey sat with the family. The service was so good how they sent her home. It was time to see Benita body for the last time and Tashione could not handle it no more she let the tears fall. Tashione lean down and gave her a kiss; Necey and Soul took off their friendship ring, put them on Benita hand, and walked away. After the service, they all went to the gravesite and it started raining. Tashione looked up and said I always knew you would go to heaven girl just look out for us down here. Everybody was leaving to go back to the house to share a meal with the family. Soul was driving the car because Tashione was a nervous wreck. They stop at Necey house so she could get some extra clothes before they went back to Soul house. Once they got there, Tashione was quiet and Necey told Soul to go check on her. Soul walked up behind Tashione and asked her are you okay girl? Tashione turned around and looked at Soul with tears running down her face and said yeah girl just give me a minute to get myself together. Soul turned around and went to the kitchen. The telephone rung and everybody jumped, Tashione answered the phone, and it was Raul asking how she was holding up? Tashione asked Raul why he was calling because he does not care about nobody but himself. I really wish you would believe when I say I do love you Tashione; I know I fucked up but hey everybody make mistakes. I hear you Raul; but did you learn from them as well? Look I have to go and please do not call me any more. (Click) Necey was laughing her ass off because she knew her girl was going to be okay. Soul asked them what you will want to do. Tashione said let us watch some movies and pop some popcorn. Everybody agreed and went to handle a small task before the movie start. Once they all got back in the living room Soul told, Tashione not any of that love shit either. Tashione said okay and the Five Heartbeats came on. Necey and Soul knew that was Benita favorite movie and did not say a word. Necey lay down on the floor and Tashione did to. Soul refused to get down so she lay on the couch smoking a blunt. Right when the movie was getting good Soul and Tashione fell asleep, leaving Necey up by herself. She kept hearing noises outside, but she did not pay too much attention until she heard something at the window. When she stood up, she did not see the dark shadow at the window with a gun pointed right for her. Necey moved just in time, the bullet caught her in the left arm, and she screamed. Tashione and Soul jumped up and seen all the blood and the window broke and turned to help Necey. Tashione ran for her gun and went to the door. She heard someone running and she begin to open fire. She thought she heard someone yell but was not for sure. Soul was on the telephone talking to the police now and told them that they were on their way to the hospital and for them to meet there. Necey was crying while Tashione was trying to comfort her. When they arrived at the hospital, Necey was rushed straight to X-Rays. Soul and Tashione was giving the nurse all Necey information. While waiting for Necey to come out of X-Rays the police came in. They started asking all kinds of questions but neither one of them had answers too. Necey Doctor was coming out and told Tashione that their friend did not make it. Soul was very upset and asking how she died, it was only a gunshot wound to the arm? Dr. Gilmore said the bullet traveled and hit her heart. Tashione was crying and Soul hugged her. The police officer told the Doctor to put an alert out for a gun wound stray. Tashione asked can they see her now. The Doctor told them to follow him and once he got to the door, he opens it for them to go in. When they went in Necey looked so peaceful it was almost as if she was sleeping. Tashione went to the body and kiss Necey on the forehead saying good-bye while Soul was up in the corner crying. When they left the hospital, both girls were in a trance. Neither could understand what was going on. Once they got to the house, Soul was very paranoid and Tashione was trying to lock the windows and doors. Tashione called Necey family to let them know what happen and what they wanted them to do. When Tashione hung the phone up, she told Soul that Mr. & Ms. Martin was on their way over and they would discuss it then. Soul went to the kitchen and put some coffee on. An hour later Necey parents was knocking at the door. Tashione opened the door and could tell that they have been crying. Once they were seated, Soul asked did they want some coffee or tea to drink? Ms. Martin said please and brings something a little stronger for my husband. When Soul came back, in the room, she passed the drinks out and they discuss the funeral arrangements, then Necey parents left. Tashione went to put the cups up in the kitchen and then the telephone rung but nobody said anything so Tashione hung up. When Tashione got back in the living room Soul asked who was on the phone? Tashione said they just hung up. Both of them were so stressed and paranoid that every little noise had them scared. The doorbell rung and it was Detective Green. Soul invited him in and Tashione asked did he want something to drink? I would like a cup of coffee if you do not mind. While Tashione was fixing the coffee Soul, begin to ask a lot of question about Benita's case. Detective Green said we are still working on it. Tashione came in with the coffee, pass everybody a cup, and sat down. Det. Green sat down, took several sips, and started asking question about what happen. After he got all the information and answered their question, he wanted to see Tashione registration for the gun. Tashione got up, went in her purse, and handed him her papers. Once he looked it over, he reached it back to her. He also told them that he found a trail of blood and that he had people out there gathering up evidence. Tashione asked the Detective why is this happening. To be honest I really don't know but I will find out, but until then there is a sick bastard out there and I want you to be careful.

CHAPTER 9

I put an alert out to all the hospital for a gun wound stray and if they go to a hospital, I will know about it. Soul was crying now and Detective Green said he needed to get back to work. Tashione walked him to the door and he asked her was Necey dating anybody? Yes, she was and gave up the name and address but also told him they had broken up a couple weeks ago. Once Tashione got back in the room Soul told her, she did not want to die. Tashione hugged her, saying you won't girl, and rocked her. Detective Green was on his cell phone telling someone on the other line that he wanted two men out here to protect the ladies because he felt they was the key to this whole puzzle. Neither one of them sleep well, when Soul went to get some coffee going she seen a strange man outside the window and screamed. Tashione came in with her gun ready to shot the first thing moving. The man outside told them that he was a police officer and he was just putting up the camera. Tashione put the gun down and there was knocking at the door. When she asked who was there and Det. Green answered, she opened the door. When he seen the sad and gloomy look in her eyes he wanted to hold her and tell her that everything is going to be all right. He told her that he had some people out here working and that he will protect her to the best of his ability and she smiled inviting him in. Soul came in and said hello. The officer that was outside came to the front door and Soul was looking hard. She went and personally introduces herself to him and Tashione started laughing. Once they got all the business done it was time for them to leave and Soul was sad looking. Tashione asked Soul what she wanted to do now. Soul said girl I do not know but I am freaking out here. Raul was at one of his old girlfriend house with his arm wrapped up. When Diamond walk in her apartment she was shocked and scared. Diamond has not seen Raul since she started nursing school and knew the only time he came around was when he needed money. Raul got up from the chair and walked up to Diamond and said I miss you baby and gave her a hug. When Diamond put her arms around Raul to hug him he winced in pain. What the fuck is wrong with you Raul? Raul was breaking out in a sweat and passed out. Diamond took off Raul shirt and seen that his arm was bandaged up so she undid it and found a gun shot wound. She cleans it up, put new ones on it, and waited for him to come through. Several hours later Raul was waking up and Diamond was right there to find out what happen to him. Raul gave her a story that someone tried to rob him and then shot him. Well listen baby; I have to go get some things from the grocery store for you so I will be right back. An hour later Diamond came in the door to hear Raul asking her where she been. Diamond looked at him and said look I have a job; and I had to go by there to get someone to cover for me. Here is some pain medicine for your ass, do not ever talk to me like that again understand. Diamond walk pass him to get him something to drink so he could take his medicine. Well I will help you out till you get back right okay. But you know I will not baby-sit your ass for long and leaned down to kiss him. When Diamond pulled away, she told Raul that she was going to take a shower and then cook them something to eat. Diamond finally got out the shower and all she had on was a robe now. When she came out she asked Raul what do you want to eat? Raul smiled and pulled Diamond down on the couch and they started kissing. She untied her robe so her breast was showing; Raul started sucking on the left nipple then going to the right one. Diamond started to moan then she unzipped Raul pants to caress his dick so he could be on her level. They both got up and went to the bedroom and Diamond lay across the bed and spread her legs open. Come and get your food baby and trust me I will feed you all the pussy you can stand. Raul got on the bed and winced with pain, so Diamond got on top of him instead. She spread her pussy so Raul can suck and lick on her clit without having to deal with the pain. Once Raul clamps down and was just sucking on her clit Diamond was grinding and moaning now. Diamond was cumin all over Raul face while saying his name while her body trembled. Diamond tried to get up but Raul was still sucking on her clit having Diamond begging him to stop. When Raul stopped, Diamond position herself over him to suck his dick. He was not in the mood now because his arm was hurting and she would do a half ass job. Look Diamond just gets up because I am not in the mood. Diamond was hurt and mad all at the same time so she got up cursing his ass out. She knew Raul always spoke his mind and she knew he was hurt so she let the statement slide. Raul saw the hurt look on her face so he encouraged her to suck his dick. First Diamond took her tongue and caresses the tip of his dick, taking her tongue and licking the split in his dick. She felt him begin to relax and she took in more and her hand begins to caress the shaft of his dick. Raul was encouraging Diamond to take it all and when she did, Raul said "Good Lord Baby"! Diamond sucked and deep throats his dick until he spilled his seed in her mouth. Diamond felt his warm cum hit the back of her throat. When they got finish, Diamond lie across Raul chest and fell asleep. Raul was thinking of what he can do next. Tashione and Soul was tired of waiting for the bodyguards to show up so Soul went to take her a shower. Tashione got on the phone to call the Detective to see why it was taking so long. While she was waiting for him to answer, her mind got to wondering who could have killed Necey. Detective Green here and Tashione said hello. Detective Green thought something was wrong at first, but he asked her was she okay. Yes, I am fine just scared as hell and want the bodyguard here that is all. Before Detective Green could say something else, Tashione heard Soul screaming and drop the phone. Detective Green grabbed his jacket and rush out of his office to the car heading to Soul's house. When Tashione got to Soul to see why she was screaming; Soul told her that a man was walking by the window. Tashione told Soul to get dress and come with her. By the time Tashione got back to the telephone, it was just beeping so she put it back on the line. By the time, Soul picked up the phone the doorbell rung and it was Det. Green coming in with his gun out. He was asking them are you okay? Soul just nodded her head while Tashione said yes. Soul walked up to him and told him that she seen a man walking by the window. Det. Green asked can he use the phone and when he did, it was quick and short. Both women watched him the whole time until he was done; he told the women that it was their bodyguards that is all... He hung the phone up and told them they should be making their presence known any minute now. Soul walked off to put some clothes on, while Tashione asked Det. Green did he want something to drink. He told her to call him Robert and he reached for her hand to bring it to his lips. Tashione just smiled saying it is a pleasure. Tashione mind begin to say more, but Robert let go and pulled Tashione body closer to his and kissed her very gently.

The doorbell rung and Tashione jumped and the spell was broken. When she opened the door there was two uniformed officers saying hello to Det. Green. Soul came down and Robert introduced them to the officers. Soul felt safer since she knew cops would be out there watching over them while they are at home. The officers made their exit and Tashione walked Robert to the door, leaving Soul to watch the intimate scene where Det. Green kissed Tashione very passionate and then told her to call him. Tashione closed the door and Soul is on her ass for the dirt. Tashione did not feel comfortable about Detective Green, but told Soul he is okay. They both bust out laughing. Soul told Tashione that she made a pallet in the living room for them to sleep. That is cool and I can go ahead and take me a shower before we lay it down. Soul was already laying on her back smoking a blunt when Tashione walked in; Soul passed her the blunt and Tashione sat down on the floor. Soul nodded off to sleep, while Tashione could not fall to sleep. Tashione finished smoking the blunt and got up to sit near the window to recall her past again. (Past) Tony was bringing Tashione home from the hospital today. Cinnamon was getting the room ready for her so she would not have to do it at the last minute. A few minutes later Tony was, carrying Tashione inside the house and everybody was saying hello to her all at once. Tony asked her do she want to sit out in the living room or go lay down. Tashione told him that she wanted to lie down. Cinnamon walked ahead of them and got the covers pulled back; so Tony laid her down and Tashione started to cry. Oh, baby do not cry because you can still have more kids. Tony pulled her into his arms and held her until she fell asleep. Tony got up and left the room and told his mother that he felt very bad and that he wanted this baby so bad. Cinnamon told him they will have more kids soon. Several hours later Tashione got up to use the bathroom and Tony was right by her side to help her. After two weeks of being, pampered Tashione was ready to go back to school and move on. Tony became very distant and cruel toward Tashione. They begin to fight and argue almost everyday and night. One night Tony was so mad that he had everybody walking around on eggshells. When dinner was over nobody moved until Tony got up from the table. Tashione was mad herself; because of the way, Tony was acting and treating everybody. She got up the nerve to asked Tony what is his damn problem? Tony looked at her and walked off.

All the kids left the room and Tashione started cursing Tony out in Spanish. When she called him a pathetic son-of-a-bitch! That got his attention; he grabbed her by the arm and dragged her to their bedroom. Once inside he slapped Tashione so hard that she fell against the wall. He picked her up by the neck and dropped her on the bed. Tony had gone crazy for a minute; choking Tashione until her face turned red. Tashione was clawing at his arm, but he still would not let go. Tashione could not hold on any more and her eyes were closing. Then all of a sudden Tony hands let go and he was fussing with a man. Tony was mad as a ragging bull so he walked out slamming the door. Tony senior grabbed Tashione and hugged her asking was she all right? Cinnamon came in the room with a glass of water. Tashione took several sips before she said yes. She got up and said give a couple of minutes to get myself together; and I will join you in the living room. By the time, Tashione got in the living room; Tony was coming in the door high as hell and drunk. When he called Tashione name, she would not answer him and that made him even madder. He walked to her and she stood up to face him. Tony went to swing at her but his father grabbed his arm and said no more. Tony was talking shit to his father and then told him that he was the man of this house. You are nothing but a stranger in this house. You have no right to just walk back in here when you feel like it. Tony father slapped him in the face. Cinnamon and Tashione just knew they were going to fight, but they did not. Tony looked at his father and started crying. Tony senior grabbed his son in his arms; and told him just because you lost your baby do not give him the right to beat on someone. In addition, it damn sure does not make you a man or make you look good. Tony senior told his son to sit down so he could explain why he was not living in the house with them. Once everybody was sitting he told his son that he could never live in New York because he got in some trouble when he was younger. And to keep him from going to jail for the rest of his life; he agreed to leave the state. Now son I want you to be the man of this house, but do not ever let me hear or see you beating a woman again. Son do you love Tashione? Yes, I do love her, why? Well show her that you love her and stop beating on her before you lose her just as I lost your mother. Tony looked at his mother and seen the tears falling down her cheeks. Tony walked toward Tashione reaching a hand to her. At first, she jumped then looked in his eyes. She seen the gentle side and took his hand and they went in their bedroom. When they got in the room, Tony hugged and kissed her. Tashione was not feeling it no more and pushed Tony away. Oh, you think I am going to fall for it again! Hell no! You act like you is the only one who lost someone. Hell, I carried that baby under my heart. When our baby died, you died with it. Tony you changed for the worst and I do not know if I can stay with you any more. I am tired of fighting with you and grieving for my baby alone. All at the same time, Tony begged Tashione not to leave him that he would change. She told him one more chance and that is it Tony. Weeks went by and Tony was acting all good and showing affection to her. They even tried to make another baby. Tashione still did not return to the hang out or the gang. She was very serious about making a baby. Tony was very anxious to create one, because he knew it would tie her to him for life. Several months went by and Tony asked Tashione one night what was she doing? Tashione told him taking a test to see if I am pregnant. Tony jumped off the bed and asked how long do we have to wait? Hold on baby it takes a few minutes. By the time, Tony got undressed Tashione said it was negative. Tony pulled Tashione on the bed and said "oh well let's keep trying" and they made love twice that night before sleep claim both of them. When morning came, Tony was ready to make love again and Tashione got mad; because all he wanted was a baby. When Tashione told him no, he got upset and started asking her what is your fucking problem. You know that is the only way we is going to have a baby. Tony, I do not want to have a baby right now. I want to finish school first and get me a job; so I can help take care of us. I do not want to live with your mother for the rest of our life. Tony was upset now, because he jumped on Tashione and beat her as if she was a man. Tashione was screaming and when she got away from him; she started throwing their pictures out the window and the jewelry. When Tony made it to her, he opens the window higher and tried to push Tashione out until she kneed him in his balls and he fell back some screaming. Tashione grabbed a pair of pants and a sweatshirt and went in the bathroom to put her clothes on. When she came out Tony was still on the floor holding his balls cursing her out. Tashione started packing her clothes, but Tony was screaming where the hell do you think your going? Tashione would not answer and when Tony got up, they started back fighting. Tashione told Tony it was over and threw him back his ring. Tony told her she was not going anywhere unless it was in a body bag. Well I guess I will be going in a body bag, but I am still leaving your ass. Tony went ape crazy and Tashione stood there and took that ass kicking without hitting back or screaming out. Tony stop and she asked him was he finish and he told her to go clean herself and this room by the time he get back. Licet had told her mother what happen when she came home from work. Cinnamon went in their bedroom and seen Tashione face all messed up and said I will help you get away. I need you to give me some time to come up with the extra money. Tashione said thank you and hugged her. When Tony came home he went to his room and seen it was clean and Tashione asleep across the bed. I got your favorite so get up and come eat. I am not going out there with my face looking like this. Tony left the room and came back with her a plate of food fixed and told her to eat. Tashione sat up and asked Tony did he like what you see? Tony just put his head down and walked out the room. Later on Tony said he was going to the hide out and he will be back in an hour or two. Tashione didn't say anything and Tony warned her if she left, he would kill her. If I cannot have you, no one else would either! In addition, he left. Thirty minutes went by and Cinnamon came in the room with two suitcases and help Tashione pack her things. She called a cab and told her to get away as far as she could. I am going to my grandmother house out in Queens and I will call you once I get there. Thank you so much for helping me, and then gave Cinnamon a hug. Cinnamon went back to the apartment and sat down as if it was a normal day. When the kids came in, she made them take a bath and get ready for dinner. Right before Cinnamon was done cooking Tony came in and went to his room. When he notices Tashione and her clothes gone, he ran to his mother and asked where is she? Cinnamon told him nobody was here when I got home. Tony cursed and took off. Tony searched everywhere except for the one place she was at. When Tashione face and bruises went away, she left the city of New York. She moved to South Carolina to where her birth mother lived. Tashione went back to school and tried to get her old life behind her, but she still dreamed of the past. Once Tashione graduated from school, three years later she went back to New York. Her family was so glad to see her and the changes. Tashione went outside with her sister

Amise and ran into Licet. When Tashione called Licet name, she stood there looking like who is you? But when Tashione made her presence known Licet ran and hugged her. Tashione and Licet talked for an hour before she said she had to go home. Tashione asked how Tony was doing. Licet told Tashione that Tony has two sons, Tashione heart dropped. Well girl you go on to the house and tell your mother I said hello and I miss her. Licet left and Amise asked her was she alright? Tashione smiled and said let us go. They went back around the old way to visit the posse and Jazz was still looking good. They hugged and talked for a while catching up on what they missed out on each other life. It was getting late so she gave her hugs and said her goodbye's. While they was walking home they seen a man sitting on a car and did not pay his ass any attention at first. The man on the car said Tashione name, and she knew the voice and stop dead in her tracks. Just hearing Tony voice made her nervous, but she stop anyway. Amise said I will wait over there for you. Tashione said no go ahead to the house I will be okay. Tony got down and held his arms out to Tashione and she went willingly. While they hugged, he said you look good. Tashione pulled back some and said thanks and so do you. He asked her all kinds of questions and Tashione answered them all truthfully, except for the part about his mama helping her to escape. Tashione asked Tony can she see a picture of his sons, he reached in his back pocket and pulled out a wallet and pulled out the pictures of his sons. Right before her eyes were the man she was so in love with smiling with two little boys. Tashione reached him the picture back with tears rolling down her face. Tony put the pictures up and pulled Tashione in his arms to hold her. He lifts her face up to kiss the tears away and told her it is okay that he always loved her. Tashione told him she has always loved him to and never stop, he gave her the end part of his shirt to dry her face up. He asked her did she have any kids of her own. Tashione said no I do not have any kids or a man in my life that is serious.

CHAPTER 10

Tony started back asking all kinds of questions about where she lived and what she does for a living. Once all Tony's question was answered he looked at her like" wow "you a welder. He even asked her do she still pack. Tashione looked at Tony like now you know I do! In addition, they both laughed. It got real quiet and Tashione asked Tony are you happy? Tony didn't say anything at first, then he looked Tashione in her eyes and told her no. I am not happy but I do love my sons' mother for giving me my sons. Tashione told Tony she always wonder how things would have been if they were still together. Tony said I guess we will never find out! Tashione said Tony I am about to go on in because I am getting a little tired. Well I got to go any way so come here and give me a hug so I can go. Once they hugged and said their goodbye's he open his car door to leave; with Tashione turning her back to leave to. Tony called her name and asked her can you ever forgive me? Tashione walked up to him and said hey I been forgave you and leaned down to kiss him and walked off. Tony got in his car and rolled the window down to tell her if you ever need me, you know where to find me. Tashione said thanks and left. Once in the house everybody asked was she okay and Tashione said yes I am okay; just had to put some closure on my past. Tashione told her family that she was going to get her some rest and to call her when dinner was ready. Tashione was on vacation for two weeks and she was ready to go on a shopping spree. They cookout with the family, they even went to a couple of clubs together. Tashione and her sisters went to the Crystal Ball Club and there they seen Tony and some of his friends. Amise told Imani she had a bad feeling since Tony is here at the club. Imani asked Tashione was she packing? Yes, I am packing why? Because Tony is over there watching you with a mean face. Tashione told her sisters not to worry about Tony because she was there to party. Some guy walked up to her and asked for a dance, which she took his hands and they headed for the dance floor. After a couple of songs Tashione wanted something to drink so she excuse herself and went to the bar to get a gin and juice.

While Tony was in the back getting mad as hell, Tashione was having a ball. By the time, another person asked her to dance Tashione had her buzz on and the guy notice this. Tashione was dancing real close and the guy put his hands on Tashione ass and Tony flipped out. He walked up to the guy and grabbed his arm, making him turn around so he could punch him in his face and broke the man's nose. Blood splattered all over Tashione face and she freaked out. Tony and his friends were fighting when Amise and Imani grabbed Tashione's arm to get her out the way. Before that could happen, someone had a hand full of her hair. Tashione was screaming out for her sisters to let her go; when they did Tashione seen, some girl was holding her hair. Tashione reached for her gun and popped the girl in the face with it. The girl grabbed her face screaming and then it seem like everybody was in the club fighting. Some other girl pulled a blade out and tried to stab Tashione in the face, but instead got her in the hand. Tashione screamed and Tony was right there by her side. Tashione grabbed Tony's headband to wrap it around her hand as tight as she could stand it. She pushed Tony out the way and went to that girl ass. Tashione got the girl on the ground and ended up scraping her left hand knuckles and then banging the girl head on the ground. Her sisters could not do anything so they called Tony to get Tashione. By then Tashione had her gun pointing it to the girl head. Tony said Tashione do not do it! By this time the fighting had slowed down and people was looking at her. Tony walked up to her and said it is over baby; and took the gun from her hand. He reached for her and they started walking outside. Tony told Tashione that he knew she was a different person because the old one would have pulled the trigger and thought nothing of it. Imani walked up and seen all the blood on Tashione and said baby you are not to blame yourself for this. Shit just happens! Tashione turned toward Tony and said what the hell is your problem? I am not your woman no more. We both had moved on with our lives. Shit Tony you have two beautiful sons that need their father alive not dead. Tony yelled out you moved on without me, hell you left me! What the fuck was I suppose to do? Wait for you to kill me! Tony you and I both know you would have beat me every chance you got till I was nothing but an empty shell. Right Tony! Look baby I could not stand there and watch another man put his hand on you. Tony suggest he give us a ride home and I said yes. He drove and nobody said a word till they got out the car. Tony even walked them to the door and Tashione invited him in while she cleaned up some. Tony was looking at the pictures on the wall and when he seen Tashione graduation picture he just smiled to himself. He even saw the one of them together, that they took at Coney Island Park. Tony was remembering how much he still miss those days and Tashione. When Tashione walked in she watched Tony for a few minutes, before she made her presence known. Tony put the picture down and told Tashione I miss you so much. Tashione told Tony that he had to let go of her. I cannot let go, I still love you and want you. Tashione knew deep down that she will always love him no matter what happen in the past, but she knew she could not turn things back. Tashione asked Tony who was his kid's mother? Tony put his head down and said nothing at first, but mumbled out Puddin name. Tashione looked at him like he was crazy then slapped the shit out of him. Get the fuck out my house and I never want to see you again, go home to your family Tony. Tashione asked him how could he after everything they went through because of her. You know what; do not even answer that because that is the past. Tony told Tashione after she left he got buck wild fucking this and that girl. I went to a club and got drunk as hell and next thing I remember I was in bed with Puddin. Well go back and get in the bed with her and take care of your family. Tony walked to the door and reached in his pocket and pulled out his mother engagement ring and said this belong to you. Tashione looked at the ring and wanted to cry but she did not. Tashione told Tony to give it to his oldest son when he is old enough. Tashione told Tony to wait a minute she had something for him. She went to her room and when she came back up front, she reached Tony his chain. I have kept this long enough and you should give it to Tony junior. Tony grabbed the chain and put the ring on the chain and Tashione helped him to clasp it on. She kissed Tony goodbye and he told her if you ever need me for anything just call me. I will come no matter what I promise you this on my name Tony. Tashione said I know and if you need me just call me. Tony told her she need to go by his mother house for a visit. I am tomorrow so tell her to be looking out for me in the morning. Later on that night, Tashione could not sleep, she thought about what she had in South Carolina and that did not add up to much. She thought about what she had in New York, which were her family and Tony if she choose to have him. Tashione asked God to give her a sign so she know what to do. She got up and cut the radio on and listened to the Quiet Storm and thought about Tony. She wondered did she want to let him go for good, so she decided to stay for a couple more weeks just to see if Tony was where she wanted to be. The next morning Tashione went to Tony's mother house. Instead of knocking on the door, she walked right in yelling out ma where are you? Cinnamon came from the back and said oh my God; look at my baby all grown up now. They hugged for minute before sitting down to talk. Tashione told Cinnamon that she knew she should have been visit, but was scared to see Tony

CHAPTER 11

Girl Tony still stay with me in the same room to. As a matter of fact, he is in the bed sleeping, go ahead, and talk to him. I can still see the love in your eyes for him. Cinnamon told Tashione that she had to leave for work and that she wanted to talk to her when she got off. I will be here mama and started walking toward Tony bedroom. When she got to the door and opened it, she saw that Tony did not change anything. She notices the chain and the ring were draped on their picture. Tashione took off all her clothes and got in the bed. Tony felt someone get in his bed and turned and seen Tashione pulled her closer to him. Please do not say a word to spoil the moment. Tony got up and brushed his teeth washed his face before getting back in the bed. Tony looked down at Tashione and seen that she still sucks on a pacifier and tried to take it from her. They laughed and played till it later turned to making love to each other. He could not get enough of her so he started back kissing her. An hour later he got up to get a washcloth to clean Tashione up. He spread her legs wide and took his tongue and licked her clit. Tashione moaned and pulled him closer to her. She begins to feel her body tremble as Tony went faster. Tashione was at her peck to climax when Tony gripped her legs. Tashione knew then that he was not going to let her push his head away when she busts a nut. Her body tensed up and then she started cumin, calling out his name. Tony did not stop till he had her begging him to stop. Tony lifted his head and Tashione legs were so weak that they were shaking. Tony came up and kissed her slow and passionate. Do you know I have dreamed of this ever since you left me, I love you Tashione. I have always loved you Tony and I want this too. Tony knew what she wanted and slides his dick inside her pussy. Damn girl you is still small just like you was before. While Tony was grinding, Tashione was meeting his every stroke. It became so intense that Tashione wrapped her legs around his waist and palm his ass. Tony said damn baby you feel so good! Tashione asked him to stop so she can ride his big dick. Which of course, he did and laid on his back. Tashione kissed his legs all the way, up till she reached his dick. She sat up and rubbed the tip of his dick across her pussy. Tony watched the woman he loved with his entire heart ride his dick. Tashione notice that he was watching and winked her eye at him and he started laughing. She took his dick in her hand to help guide it in. When that was done, she told Tony not to touch her and to keep his hands above his head. He said okay baby; work your magic on me. While Tashione was riding his dick, he had to grab something, so he gripped the headboard. She did all kinds of things to him to drive him wild and begging for release. She never took her eyes off him while she tightens up her pussy muscle around his dick. Tony was making all kinds of ugly faces and Tashione wanted to laugh at him; but knew it would spoil the moment so she held it in. She had him calling out her name, then she grabbed his balls gently and he went crazy. He flipped her ass over and went to pounding the pussy till they both climax together. Tony got up and Tashione turned over on her back and put her pacifier in her mouth so she could go to sleep. He kissed her on her back and lay down beside her. She turned over to lie in his arms and said I love you, but where does this leave us? How about we take one day at a time and slowly this time. Baby I never let Puddin in my bed and I want you to meet my sons. Tashione said okay, then the phone rung. Tashione picked it up and said hello. There was a woman on the other line asking to speak to Tony; so she reached him the phone. Tony was fussing at her and Tashione grabbed the phone asking who this is? No bitch, who is this? Do not worry who this is, just state your business? Puddin was cursing and carrying on that it was getting on her nerves. Tashione told Tony to do something with your play toy real quick. Puddin heard and knew right then that it was Tashione. So Tony what is she doing there? (Click). The phone rung again and this time Tashione told her that she was back to stay and her and Tony are getting back together. (Click) Later on, that night Tashione went home and Rosa was concerned and told her that Mark had called. Tashione got on the phone and dialed his number. Mark was so happy to hear her voice that he could not tell she was being cold and dry towards him. When are you coming home baby? Tashione told him soon. Every time Mark said something mushy, all she could do was say me too. He never comments on it even though he felt it in his heart that he was losing her to her ex-boyfriend. Mark told her to call him tomorrow and hung up. Tashione went in the living room and turned the radio on and El Debarge song called "Love me in a special way" was playing and she had choices to make about her feelings for Tony and Mark. Mama Rosa came in and hugged her, telling Tashione it is going to be alright. I want you to think long and hard about whom you want to be with; and I mean everything to baby from good and bad. Tashione started crying and pouring her heart out to her mama. She told her mother that she cared about Mark, but Tony was her heart and that she was scared he might hurt her again and plus he has two sons. Ma it is by a woman I shot many years ago. Rosa told her if she loved Tony like she thought she did then his sons should not matter at all. Rose kissed Tashione and said you do what make's you happy because only you can live your life. Tashione said good night ma and thanks. She went to bed a few minutes later and still did not know what to do. Her father was yelling for her to get up and she could not move at all. When she did get up out the bed, it was almost noon and took her shower. She realized that she could not leave Tony alone and put all the hurt and pain of her losing the baby in the past. She called Tony and told him she was on her way over and hung up. When she got there, she notices that Puddin was there with the boys. Tony gave Tashione a kiss and said I want you meet my sons. Puddin was very upset, while the boys looking like who is this lady my daddy is kissing. Tony called his sons over and told them who Tashione was and that they have been friends for a long time. Tashione thought that the boys were very polite. Tony junior said she's pretty daddy, before he was told to go to the room and play. The boys wanted to stay but when their father told them it was grown up time to talk they left without saying another word. As soon as the boys were gone Puddin started going off about she did not want this bitch around her sons. She went to slap Tony but Tashione stop her. Tashione said look I am not going to put up with your bullshit, me and Tony decided to get back together and that is all you need to know. Puddin said what about your sons Tony? Tony said I will always take care of my sons and be there for them. Puddin said oh hell no! You will not play family man with my sons and called the boys so they could leave. Tony was looking all confused because they did not talk about none of this and he wanted his sons. Tashione seen the puzzled look and pulled him into her arms; saying baby we are going to handle this together but you got to trust me. Tony said sure baby, but he still was not convinced. Tony sat down on the chair and rubbed his hands over his face and through his hair. Tashione walked over to Tony and squat down and hugged him. Tony told her that he did not want to lose his sons and if Puddin would try to come between that, he would hurt her. She looked in his eyes and said I know you would baby, but just trust me on this. Tashione got up and pulled out her cell phone dialing her lawyer's number. She asked Tony what is Puddin real name? It is Carmen Lopez , and why you need to know? Hi, Tommy this is Tashione and I need a favor and started to explain the whole situation to him. A few minutes later Tommy told her okay and that, he would start working on it and call her back. (Click) She told Tony that Tommy is going to work on it but we need a car and a house to get the boys. So when do you want to go shopping for a house? Tony looked and said damn baby you work fast, but I love you for it. Tashione was looking through the newspaper for a house when she found a four bedroom with two bathrooms in Queens New York for rent. Tashione called to set up an appointment for 1:00p.m... That gave Tony enough time to take a shower and have lunch as well. The sex can wait till everything was done and over. When they got to Queens, they did not have a hard time finding the house. It was beautiful to Tashione, but Tony said it was too big for him. While the lady was showing it to them, Tashione did all the talking and Tony just listened. I love this house so how much is the rent? The realtor lady said the rent was seven hundred dollars and the deposit was Five hundred dollars. Tony was about to say hell no, but Tashione pulled Tony to the side and said baby we need this for the boys. Tashione turned around and said we will take it. The lady said all I need is the deposit and your signature and I will give you the keys to start moving in when you like too. Tony couldn't believe his ears, he was in shock. He asked Tashione okay we got the house but my income will not take care of the rent. Look baby you and me as a team can do anything just have faith. How about I pay the rent and you take what ever bill you want. He did not like the sound of that at all, but went along with it. I need to call Tommy and let him know that we got us a house. After all that was done, Tashione said Tony make love to me right here in our new home. Tony said whatever you like, I will surely give to you. Tony picked her up and they went to the living room and started taking off each other clothes. Tashione was caressing and touching herself and that shit turned Tony ass on real bad. Tashione watched Tony take off his shirt and twirled it in the air, then slowly letting it drop to the floor. He then kicked off the sneakers and the pants came down next. Tashione was really getting into touching herself. Tony did not want to be left out and felled on the floor trying to hurry up. Tashione giggled and Tony crawled on his knees to her. When he came face to face, she pulled her finger out and put it in Tony mouth to suck her juices off. Tashione told Tony that she wanted to feel his dick in her mouth and they got in the 69 position. She begin to lick the split on the head of his dick. Tashione begin to take more and more of him in her mouth; till she could feel his dick hitting the back of her throat she gagged a couple of times. Once she got her jaw bone right it was on and popping. Tony was enjoying getting his dick sucked so much he forgot to even touch Tashione pussy. She raised up and told him he need to get busy on the pussy too, cause she wants to purr some. Tony started eating from the ass to the pussy. Which she was loving it now and grinding her pussy on Tony's face. What really took the cake was when he got on the clit and stuck his finger in her ass gradually fingered her. Tashione started to moaning and grinding even harder. Telling Tony "that's it baby"; oh shit I am cumin baby! Tashione nutted so hard that her back locked up on her and she screamed out his name. (Present) When Tashione woke up, she was hot and wet between her legs. She goes to the bathroom and washes her face and brushes her teeth. She later takes a shower and got dress. When she came down Soul was drinking a cup of coffee. Soul seems to be in another world and Tashione knew she was worried about what was going to happen to them. Tashione asked Soul are you going to work. Hell no I am going to call my boss and see if I can take a week off from work. Tashione said, I should do the same thing myself and I hope it do not be no shit either. Tashione left to go to her job and Soul was getting ready to leave when the phone rung. (Hello) straight from the top a man was talking shit. Look you was the one that fucked up not me, hold up! Just call me later. (Click) Tashione got to her job and went to her boss office to ask for a two weeks leave and explained why. Her boss was very scared for Tashione and told her if she needed anything to just let her know. Before Tashione knew it, she had talked to her boss for an hour and half about everything that was going on. Tashione said I got to go now, but I will be in touch with you. Tashione left and headed out for Det. Green office to see if anything was found out or what she's supposed to do now. She didn't have to wait long because he was motioning her to enter his office. Once inside and behind close doors he went to kiss her; and she kissed him back very slow and passionate. The telephone rung and they broke the kiss. When Det. Green answered the phone, it was one of the officers that had been following Soul. He told Detective Green that someone had tried to take Soul out, but didn't succeed because he took the hit for her. Det. Green said is you crazy, but the officer said it was okay he had on a vest. Det. Green said gather up as much evidence that you can and come to my office. Tashione was just looking at all the awards he had on his walls and smiled to herself. Det. Green told Tashione to sit down; when she was sitting in front of his desk, he told her that someone had tried to take Soul out but failed. Tashione got nervous and scared and started crying. Det Green was not used to woman crying in front of him. All he could do was get up and pull her into his arms. She was shaking so bad that it took him almost thirty minutes before he could calm her down. A few minutes later Soul and a police officer walked in the office and Tashione grabbed her friend to make sure she was alright. The men step out of the office to talk in private; so what you got? Well not much but I did get the color of the car and three shells that I took to be scanned. Det. Green said it's a start and maybe we can catch whoever this person is. While they were waiting for the information to come up, Soul was telling Tashione how the officer had caught the bullet that was meant for her. Soul was going on about how he risks his life for her; and that she had never had anybody to ever do that for her. Soul wanted to do something special for Officer Roberts. When Det. Green and Officer Roberts came back in, they were ready to question Soul about what she remembers. Soul was telling them that the guy didn't look familiar, but he had a hat pulled down low to cover the eyes. However, there was long dark hair hanging from the hat and the eyes seem to be small and almond shape. Later on Tashione and Soul decided to go grab something to eat at this nice diner called "Destiny's." While they waited to be seated, then they placed their drink order from the bar. By the time the drinks was almost gone a waitress came to seat them out on the pier. The waitress gave them the menu and asked them did they want another round of drinks. Once the waitress got the drink orders, she told them to look over the menu till she got back. A couple minutes the drinks were ready and they had made up their mind what they wanted to eat. Tashione wasn't really hungry, but kept thinking about how she was going to keep them safe. Soul kicked Tashione leg and asked her what is up? Look girl are you willing to learn how to shot a gun? Hell no! You know I don't like guns, hell I could never pull the trigger on someone else. I know you mean well Tashione but if it's my time; I will go and trust the lord. Tashione hit the table and said come on girl! Someone is trying to kill us and I'm not ready to die. I trust in the Lord but I can help protect myself to. I got my whole life to live and I'm going to see my days, with or without God help. The waitress came by and asked them did they need anything else? No, thank you; but can you bring the check please. While they was getting ready to leave Soul tapped Tashione in her side to look up. When Tashione turned she looked Raul straight in the eyes. Diamond seen Raul smiling and got a little jealous and gripped his arm a little tighter. Soul and Tashione walked by and Tashione said baby don't hold to tight. I damn sure don't want him and they started laughing while leaving the diner. Soul and Tashione got in their car and Soul asked her was she okay? Tashione said yeah girl let's roll out. Tashione cut the radio up and started singing to the song that was on. Now you know your ass got a beautiful voice and should be singing on someone label making us some money. Tashione started laughing out loud saying child please. Oh, go by my house so I can get some more of my things. Once they got to the house and she punched in the code to the alarm to cut it off. The house still had a smoke odor so they open up a couple of windows to air it out some. Girl they need to hurry up and get your shit back right. I know that's right because I can protect us a whole lot better here. Well girl let's get to cleaning some parts up, where do you want to start at? Tashione told her they can start from the top to the bottom. I need to check and see what I got as far as cleaning stuff and what I don't have we can go pick up later. Tashione went to the cleaning closet and when she opens the door, an envelope fell out. Tashione picked it up and wondered what was in it. Soul told her to open the damn envelope already! When she did, there was $ 10,000 dollars with a message that said Soul is next. Soul was trying to read the message but Tashione wasn't trying to feel it. She walked over to her purse and pulled out her cell phone dialing Det. Green number. Is there any way you could come out to my house I think you need to see something important that might help with the case. Det. Green told her he could be there in less than twenty minutes. (Click) Soul wanted to know what was going on and Tashione showed her the message on the paper. Soul face turned pale and her legs got weak. Tashione grabbed her and helped her to sit down. Det. Green knocks on the door and Tashione let him in. He asked her was everything okay and she said yes, but I found this in my cleaning closet and reached him the paper. After reading it, he asked her does Soul know. Yes, I showed it to her and she is sick now. I got her sitting down at the table in the kitchen. Det. Green said; oh my God we had that sick bastard right under our nose and didn't know it. Tashione told Soul that Raul is behind the murders and she tripped. Tashione didn't understand why he was doing this to her or even wanted to kill her and her friends. Det. Green said I need to take the envelope and have it examine as well. Tashione didn't mention it had money in it and Soul didn't either. When Det. Green left, Tashione and Soul was like I'm going to get that bastard if that the last thing I do. Soul told Tashione that they needed a plan so they both put their heads together to plot revenge against Raul.

CHAPTER 12

Diamond and Raul was enjoying their late dinner, till Diamond got to whining about how Raul still reacts to Tashione. Raul was really getting sick of explaining how he didn't care for Tashione. He really wanted to tell her the truth, but he wasn't sure how much he could trust her. Raul was thinking about whether or not Tashione and Soul was still wondering when their time would come. He even thought about how he was going to get them. He knew that Soul love to eat, but how could he get close enough to Tashione. Diamond was calling Raul's name over and over till he responded. Raul was like what it is! Damn girl, you are getting on my nerves. His cell phone went off and when he answered it, it was Det. Green asking him to come to the station for more questions. Raul was like Damn! Raul told Diamond it was time to go. He had to make a stop by the police station before they went home. Diamond said if you ever need me to cover for you just let me know. Raul just looked at her like she was crazy; but didn't say a word but thanks baby. Diamond wasn't slow at all and she knew that Raul had killed Bonita and Necey because he talked about it in his sleep. Diamond was in love and she would do anything to protect Raul at all cost. When they got to the station, Raul asked the desk clerk to let Det. Green know that he was there to see him. Ten minutes later Det. Green asked Raul to follow him to his office. Raul reached for Diamond hand and when she touched his hand, Raul pulled her closer and said it won't take long. I want to go with you; there are no secrets between us right baby. Det. Green told them it was okay if she wanted to come. As they walked to the office, Raul was getting nervous and started to sweat some. Once inside and everybody was seated, Det. Green started asking questions about where he was on the night of February 1 and September 20? Raul told him that he knew where he was on the first and on the 20th, he was with Diamond all night. Diamond confirms his alibi and Det. Green asked him about Bonita death again. Raul told him he was in bed with Tashione when they got the news. He told Diamond he was sorry to bring up the past in front of her. Det. Green pulled out an envelope out and asked Raul have he seen this before? Raul eyes got big as hell and he knew they were on to him and that Tashione had his money. No I haven't seen it before; why do you ask this of me? Just doing my job and Raul, please don't leave town because this was far from being over with. Det Green got up and opens the door for them to leave. Raul told Diamond to come on that they needed to talk. Det. Green had Raul car bugged while he had them in his office. Diamond wanted to know what was going on now, but Raul said no let's wait baby. Diamond was very inpatient so she had Raul to stop at the mall on the way home. When they got out of the car and started walking towards the mall, Diamond pulled Raul over to the benches to sit down. Diamond looked Raul in his eyes and said start talking. Raul told Diamond that he took on a job to kill Tashione and her friends that he didn't know who the person was that was paying him to do the job. I have already killed two of them and got two left, but Tashione is going to be the hardest because she know how to protect herself. Diamond didn't say a word at first and her facial expression stayed calm. This really puzzled Raul and he didn't really know if he could trust her. So tell me how much are you being paid to do this? Well there are two prices; one for the friends is $10,000 and a million for our lucky Tashione. Diamond eyes got so big that all she seen was dollars signs. Raul finally let her in and grabbed Diamond by the neck and told her if you ever cross me, I would kill you without a second guess. When Raul let go she was panting hard and started crying saying I love you Raul and I would never do anything to hurt you. Raul was quiet now because he was thinking about his money he left at Tashione house and since Det. Green didn't say nothing about the money he knew who had it. Tashione gave Soul $2,000 dollars for pocket change and she kept the rest. Soul was like girl you don't have to give me any money. Tashione walked up to Soul and said you are my only best friend left and I love you; so let's go shopping and spend up Raul money cause he owe us. When they got back in the car and were headed toward the mall neither girls saw Raul driving by. Raul got to the house and punched in the code but nothing happen. He couldn't get inside the house without the alarm going off so he left. Once he was inside his car he started hitting the steering wheel; and cursing Tashione out for everything she was worth. Meanwhile at the mall Tashione ordered herself a new bedroom suite and living room set made out of cherry wood. She then looked at some carpet and got a deep wine color that went good with the living room suite. Soul caught up with Tashione in the electronics section where she was ordering a big screen TV. with surround sound. She told Soul that everything will be delivered this weekend. I guess this mean we will be moving to your house so you can protect us better. Tashione looked at her and said you got that right. Alright Tashione let's go so we can get back to the house and clean up before they deliver all this stuff you purchase today. When they got there, Tashione called Det. Green and asked him do he mind helping them paint. No, I don't mind helping because this way I get to spend some time with you. That is great and we can get it done in no time, can you ask the officer that help Soul to come as well. I know she will like that since that is all she talks about. I will see if he can make it okay, talk to you later. (Click) Once Tashione hung up the phone Soul was saying we need to go get some food for this house. How about you go, so I can take me a shower and tidy up here. Soul left and Tashione cleaned up some. The phone rung and Det. Green said it's a go. We will be there in two hours; do you need me to bring anything? Um no, just yourselves and some old clothes. Okay see you when we get there. (Click) Soul was pulling up in the drive way with bags in her hand, calling out for Tashione to come help her. I'm coming girl; give me a chance to get to you. So where are we going to cook the food? How about the grill and this way we could chill out here on the patio and talk. By the time dinner got done, the phone was ringing and it was Det. Green. Um Tashione I will be there in an hour, but Officer Roberts will be late. Tashione said okay and hung up the phone. (click) Soul was in the kitchen doing some last minute details and just singing her non singing butt off. Tashione was happy to see her friend smiling and being happy. Well an hour later passed and the door bell rung, Soul said she got it while Tashione was getting ready for her new friend. Soul opened the door and all she seen was Det. Green and her face expression drop. Oh don't worry Officer Roberts is running late. Well come on in to the living room and have a seat while Tashione comes down. Det. Green watched as Tashione came down the spiral stairs. When she came face to face, he stood up and reached her a bottle of wine for dinner. Well how about we all go to the patio and have drinks till Officer Roberts comes. Tashione led the way and Det. Green watched her ass the whole time. When he notice Soul watching him he tried to cough to cover it up Soul went to the cabinets to get three glasses down so Det. Green could pour everyone a drink. The door bell rung again and Soul asked Tashione to answer it because she was nervous. Girl you know I got your back so just chill okay honey. No, I think I should answer the door instead. What ever girl but don't keep him waiting. Before Soul opens the door, she checked her hair and appearance before saying who it is. Raul said open the damn door bitch! I came to talk to Tashione. Soul called out Tashione named and when she came up front she seen Raul standing there. What the fuck are you doing at my house? We have nothing to talk about so get your ass off my property before something bad happen to you. Oh, before I forget I had your shit packed up and mailed to your address, so holla nigga. Raul was getting mad because he really needed to get in the house to get the rest of his money before they find that. Tashione went to close the door; but Raul put his foot in the way and called Tashione name out again. What the hell is it? Raul was about to go off when he seen Det. Green coming to the door. Which Soul went and told him they had an unwanted guest. Raul said I will talk to you some other time and turned to leave and walked right up on Officer Roberts. Who everybody said hello too. Once everybody was inside and sitting at the table, Soul and Tashione was putting the plates and food on the table. Tashione asked Det. Green to say grace. Once that was done they begin passing the food around. Soul asked the gentlemen was everything okay and they both said yes at the same time. Officer Roberts told Soul to call him Keith from now on. Keith and Soul talked about all kinds of things and didn't pay any attention to Tashione and Det. Green. Soul asked him why he was not married yet. Well I have not found the right woman yet to settle down with. Do you want some more wine? No but I would like to go outside to talk more with you, if you don't mind the company. Soul light up like a damn Christmas tree. They went outside and Soul grabbed her wine glass and winked at Tashione. Keith asked Soul why she's not married and with children running around her legs. Soul smiled. What are you looking for in a man and a relationship? Well for starters honesty, humor, security, communication, and love. Soul got up and told him she will be right back. When she came back, she reached inside her pocketbook and pulled out a box that was gift wrapped. This is for saving my life and I hope you like it. Keith was shocked because nobody has ever done that before for him. Keith opened it up and it was a pin with a guardian angel and on back, it had Soul name. Keith was so touch that he kissed Soul and she kissed him back. When they broke the kiss, Soul was smiling. So what are you doing this weekend Soul? Helping Tashione get her place back together. Oh, I forgot all about that. You could come and help if you like. I would like that very much, but I would love to spend some one on one with you. Well Keith we could do that later if you want. That's a plan I can deal with Soul. So how should I dress? Well be comfortable because I want to catch a movie and go out to eat afterwards. Don't get all razzle dazzle on me either. I promise I won't. Tashione and Det. Green was so wrapped up into their own little world that they didn't even hear when Soul and Keith came back in. Det. Green was talking to Tashione about how he admired her strength and courage; that he wanted to take her out on a date to get to know her better. I would like that very much, but there is one problem I don't even know your first name. That is no problem it's Derrick. Well nice to meet you Derrick. They both laughed. Tashione got up and started putting the dishes in the dish washer and Derrick helped her out as well. Soul said, well Tashione when do we get the pleasure of asking these nice gentlemen to help us paint your house. Derrick and Keith said we can help now if you got the stuff ready. Oh okay, it's in the closet right there by the door. Me and Soul can go ahead and put the covers on everything. Once everything was covered, everybody grabbed a brush and started painting. Three hours later, it was all done, and everybody was tired as hell. Derrick made the statement that we work well together and Soul looked at Keith and said yes we do. Keith walked over to Soul and told her that he had to be leaving, because his shift starts in a couple of hours. Soul walked him to the door and got her a goodnight kiss and a promise to call her later. She walked back to the living room and told Tashione and Derrick good night before she went upstairs for bed. Tashione asked Derrick did he want some coffee and he said no thanks, but I do need to be on my way too. Tashione walked him to the door, but before he could open it, she was pulling him in her arms for a kiss. While they were kissing, Derrick dick begins to rise and Tashione didn't seem to mind either. Derrick pulled away and said damn woman that haven't happen to me in years. I know how you are feeling because I feel the same way Derrick but it has to wait. Derrick kissed her again and walked to his car. She watched the car drive away till she couldn't see it any more. She closed and locked the door before setting the alarm. She went in search of Soul where she found her in the kitchen wiping down the counters. Soul are you okay girl? Yeah I'm okay, but I really like Keith and I think he's the one. Tashione said yeah, I know how you feel girl because I feel that way about Derrick. They both started laughing. Soul asked what we do now. Well there is not much we can do but take it one day at a time. Alright let's finish getting Raul shit out of your house so he won't have any excuse to come back. I know that's right. Both of them went upstairs to the bedroom and hit the closet up to see if any of his shit was there. Tashione haven't been in the room since the fire and it felt funny to be there now. What's up girl? Nothing I was just looking at how different the room looks since the fire. She started getting flashes of things that she couldn't put together. She shakes her head and went to help Soul out. Tashione grabbed a suit from the closet and she wondered why Raul left his expensive silk suit behind? Soul said girl what's the hold up? Tashione said this is what Raul had on at my birthday party. Soul said so what girl! However, something kept telling Tashione to check the suit out. When she did, she found more money and a list of names that was very familiar to her. Tashione told Soul to call Det. Green but Soul said it's too late and we can go there in the morning. Tashione started crying now and when Soul went to hug her; she said I know who is after us. Soul pulled back and asked who? It's Raul. How do you know this? Look Soul and she reached her the paper with the names on it. Soul looked at Tashione all shocked and said we got to get this list to Det. Green in the morning. Let's get some sleep now and handle our business in the morning okay. Yeah but do you mind sleeping in the room with me? You know I don't, it will be like the old days. They both got in the bed but could not sleep, so they talked about all the information they had and piece together the puzzle. Several hours passed and Tashione still couldn't sleep so she decided to take her shower and get dress. Soul done the same thing and they met up in the kitchen to drink some coffee. The doorbell rung around 7:00 a.m. and when Tashione asked, who is it? It's me Derrick.

Tashione opened the door and said I was about to call you. Oh yeah! Well I'm hear so what's up. Well me and Soul found this and I think it will help you out and to let you know who it is that is after us. Tashione walked to the kitchen and Derrick followed in behind saying Good morning to Soul. Tashione grabbed the list off the table and reached it to Derrick. After he looked it over, he asked her where you found this. It was in Raul suit pocket that he wore for my birthday party. I'll be monkey ass, I had that bastard in my office and let him go. Since we know who is after you I can put a watch person on him. When he make his move, we will catch his ass then. Look, he has a bug in his car and I got someone following him. He will get slack and when he does, I will be there to bust his ass. Well I got to be on my way to work and will keep a check on both you lady's. Derrick left and Tashione said okay Soul it's just you and me for right now so let's find something to do. We can go shopping if you like and spend some more of Raul money. Soul laughed and said come on let's go. Once they got in the mall, it was just what they needed to get Raul off the brains. They went in this China Restaurant to eat then headed to the grocery store to get some food for the house. Once they got back home it was 3:00 p.m. and Tashione cell phone rung. She opened it up and seen that it was Det. Green and answered it. They talked for awhile and she said okay that will be great, see you then. (Click) Tashione told Soul that Derrick and Keith will come over tonight after work. Now that's what I'm talking about! A man to protect us from Raul. That statement kind of hurt Tashione feelings but she didn't comment on it. Once they got back to the house and put everything up, they started dinner. At 5:30 p.m. both gentlemen was at the door with bags in their hands. Keith was the first to ask can he take a shower. You sure can, Soul shows him where the bathroom is, and asked Derrick do he need to take one as well. Yes that would be great; Tashione showed Derrick to her bathroom. Then laid across her bed while Derrick was in the shower. Once the men were done, they went to the kitchen to eat dinner. Derrick and Keith did the dishes for the ladies and all. Soul liked a man that knew how to clean up behind themselves. Derrick asked Tashione would it be a problem if he and Keith stayed over. Tashione told him she didn't have a problem with that; because she had extra bedrooms that they could sleep in. Soul go show Keith where he can sleep tonight and I will show Derrick his room. Everybody got up and headed upstairs. Derrick told Tashione that he could sleep on her couch, but Tashione told him no you can sleep in the bedroom across from mine. Well then, I will see you in the morning. Good night Derrick. Tashione went to her bedroom and took a shower but couldn't go to sleep. She heard a knock at her door and Derrick came in. She looked at him and said you can't sleep either? How about I hold you till you fall asleep. That would be nice, and Tashione patted the bed for him to sit on. Tashione put a pillow on his lap, while he rubbed her arm and played in her hair. Before Tashione knew it, she was going to sleep and dreaming again.

CHAPTER 13

(Past) Tashione lawyer called and set an appointment with them both. Once they got together and were discussing some things that Tony didn't know about Carmen Lopez known as pudding. Puddin has been selling drugs while the boys were at school and snort coke to with her new big time drug dealer boyfriend Brian. Tony wanted his sons out of that environment and was willing to do anything. Tommy said that he had pictures of Carmen and Brian selling dope and that they were on the police hit list. Now I have worked out everything with the police so you could pick up your boys from home; but you need to do this when they get home from school. How about I just pick my sons up now and let shit go down. No Tony that would not work because Carmen won't do anything as long as she know her sons are not in school. Two weeks went by and Tashione and Tony were moving their things into the new house. Tony was still moping around and Tashione called Tommy to see if and when shit was going to go down. Hello Tashione, I was about to call you and let you know that Tony need to call Carmen and see if he can get the boys this weekend. That would not be a problem on his part, but it might be for Carmen. I don't think it would because they got a big meeting with the undercover and she can't seem to get someone to watch the boys. Oh okay, I will call you back to let you know what happen. (Click) Tony baby I got a message for you from Tommy. Tony grabbed the phone and called Carmen, she was acting her old nasty self at first. Look pudding I want to see my sons and this shit been going on long enough. All of a sudden, her tone changed, you can come get the boys and keep them for the weekend, and I will pick them up myself from your mother house. Tony keeps that bitch of yours away from my sons. Alright pudding I will, I just want to spend time with my sons. I will be there Friday at 4:00 p.m. when they get out of school. (Click) Tashione walked over to Tony and wrapped her arms around his waist and said it's going to be okay baby, you know I love you. Tony couldn't wait to get his sons Friday, it felt like the days and nights was dragging by. When Friday morning came Tony was up and happy. Tashione was relieved to see his mood change. Tony ate breakfast while Tashione sipped on some orange juice. Tony left for work and Tashione went out to meet with a Welding Company for a job. Later on that day, she got her job and Tony should be on his way to get the boys. Well Tashione I going to start the paper work so that Tony and you will be granted custody of the boys. She thanked Tommy for everything he has done for her and would repay him back one day. Tony went to pudding house to pick his sons up. When he rung the bell pudding new boyfriend Brain answered the door mean mugging Tony. Tony asked for pudding and Brian told him to come in and have a seat. While Tony was being lead to the living room he seen a picture of them all, and that shit pissed him off. Puddin came out the back room with the boys and their bags. The boys ran to their father for some much needed hugs. Tony asked pudding what time she will be picking up the boys. Um how about you bring them back around 3:00 p.m. Sunday. Tony told the boys to say good-bye to mommy and he grabbed their bags. Puddin hugged and kissed them and Brian gave them a high five and said he would have them something special when they came home. The boys ran to their daddy and they left to get in the car. While driving to Queens Tony called Tashione and told her, he got the boys and is on their way home. Tahione called Tommy and said everything good on our part, now get Carmen. Oh, we will get her you can trust that. I got to go now the boys are here. (Click) Tashione had the boys room hooked up for them. While Tony was driving home he asked his sons was they ready to see their daddy's new crib. Tony junior asked his daddy where is your girlfriend Tashione at? Tony said she's at the house waiting on us. Tony junior said cool I like her, but Mickey was a mama boy. Once they got to the house; the boys jumped out and ran for the door. Tashione had the door open and ready for them to come in. Tony junior hugged and kissed her, and Mickey was like Hey and walked on by her. Tony was carrying the boy's bags in and gave Tashione a kiss and told her to give Mickey some time. Tony took the bags upstairs and Mickey followed him, while junior stayed with Tashione. Once Mickey seen his room he begin to smile some; he asked his daddy why he don't love mama no more? Tony pulled Mickey on his lap and said listen, I will always love your mother because she gave me you and your brother. However, me and mommy couldn't get along while we were together so we decided it was best to separate. Mickey asked do you love Tashione. Yes, son I do and I want you to love her too, so give her a chance you just might like her. Mickey said okay, but I won't call her mommy! They hugged and went back down the stairs. When they got to the kitchen Tashione asked what do you guys want to eat for dinner? The boys hurried up and said McDonalds. Tashione looked at Tony and said yeah these are your sons and started laughing. They all went to McDonalds and Tony couldn't believe his eyes, his sons had big appetites. Tashione was just eating on some French fries. Tony seen the changes in Tashione, but would bring it up later. Tashione caught Tony watching her and asked the boys do they want to go outside and play. They yelled out yeah and took off running. Tony asked Tashione what is wrong. Nothing baby, I'm fine and smiled. Tony said bullshit, you been acting strange for a couple of days now and you will tell me what's wrong. There is nothing wrong, so stop trying to make nothing into something, and walked away. When Tashione went outside, she heard the boy's arguing about her. Mickey told junior he better not call that bitch mommy. Tashione called Mickey name and he said shit and walked away. Tashione called Mickey and grabbed junior hand and followed Mickey back inside. Tashione sat junior next to Mickey and told him to listen up because I'm not going to say this but once. Tony was looking like what is going on! Mickey I'm not trying to take your mothers place. I love your father and one day me and him is going to get married and I will be your step-mother. I'm not a mean person and if you give me the chance, you will see that for yourself. All this means is that you will have two mothers that will love you unconditionally and protect you. Mickey told Tashione that if it wasn't for her that his parents would be together. Hold up Mickey; No Tony, I got this. Look at me Mickey! was your parents together when I met you at your grandmothers' house? Mickey said no. It's not because of me and I don't want you to place the blame on me. Your daddy and I was together long before your mother was. Mickey looked at his dad and asked was that true? Yes son that's true and I done some mean things to Tashione to drive her away. Look guys are you ready to go home and have a family talk. While they were on their way home, it was very quiet except for the music. Once they got to the house, everybody went to the kitchen and sat down at the table.

Tony told Mickey that he didn't want to ever hear him curse again or bully his little brother. Mickey was feeling mad now and he said that he will never call Tashione mommy; because he had a mother and wanted to go home now. Mickey ran to his room and Tony went after him. Junior didn't know what to say or do. Tony was about to open his son door when he heard Tashione call his named to come quick. Tony answered the phone and it was Puddin calling from jail. Tony was mad as hell about what Puddin had done to the boys' life. Tony I need for you bring the boys to see me and Tashione too. Tony told her that they will be there in the morning. (Click) Tashione had the feeling that Puddin was in jail now and she hugged Tony to give him the support he so much needed. Baby listen things will work out and don't push Mickey to hard he will come around. Right now, you and I must think about the boys because their mother is in jail and they are really going to need you to understand their feelings. They went to bed and didn't really say too much to each other, just held each other. Tashione got up in the morning to cook breakfast while Tony got the boys dressed. Once everybody was seated, Tony said grace and begins fixing the boys a plate. After they ate, they went to the jail house to see Puddin. The boys wanted to know why they were there, but before anyone could say something Puddin was walking in. The boys ran to their mother and hugged her real tight asking why she is here and not at home. Mickey started crying and asking a lot of questions. Puddin walked the boys to the table and sat them on her lap. She explain to them that she had to go away and that they had to live with daddy and Tashione till she come home. Mickey said he wanted to stay with her in jail. I wish you could baby, but they won't let you okay. Puddin turned to talk to Tashione now and said I know I gave you a hard time in the past; but now I need for you to help take care of my sons. I want to apologize to you and hope you can forgive me. Tashione accepted it and told her i will help in any way that I can. Puddin told the boys to be good for Tashione and they both said okay at the same time. Tony told Puddin I will bring the boys to see you every weekend. Thanks Tony and I'm sorry for all this. Tashione told Puddin to call the boys when she feels like it. The guard came in the room and said it was time to go visiting hours are over with. Puddin got up and gave the boys a hug and told them to be good that she loved them with all her heart.

Tashione grabbed Mickey and said it's going to be okay and he just bust out crying in her arms. They all left and went to Puddin house to pack up the boys stuff and put Puddin things in storage for her. When they got back to the house, the telephone was ringing and it was a Police officer at the jail house, telling them that Carmen hung herself after she was sentence to twenty-five years to prison. Tony started crying and the boys started screaming cause they seen their father fall to the floor in tears. Tashione took the phone and said hello; and was told the same thing Tony was and thanked the officer before she hung up. Tashione called Cinnamon and asked could she watch the boys and told her what happened. They got the boys back in the car and went to Cinnamon house. Tony sat the boys down and told them what happen to their mommy. Mickey was crying and hitting his daddy saying no, I want my mommy over and over. Junior really didn't understand what was going on, but when Tashione told him that mommy went to heaven to be an angel he seems to accept that more. He just sat on Tashione lap and hugged her real tight. Tony finally got Mickey to calm down and told him the same thing that Tashione told Junior. Cinnamon told them to go on and take care of things that she had the boys and they will be okay. Tony and Tashione got in the car and he was so fucking mad at Puddin for putting the boys and herself through this bullshit. When they got to the police station, a lady at the front desk gave them white envelopes that had Carmen Lopez name on it. There was several letters in it that had names on it. Tashione thanked the lady and they left. When they got back to Cinnamon house, the boys were playing with their little cousins. Tony said I need to call Puddin parents to let them know what happen. While he was on the phone with Puddin mother, she told him that she didn't want any part of it. What about your grandkids? I have never been apart of their lives and I want to keep it that way. Tony called that woman all kinds of nasty names before he hung up on her. Tony told his mother about the conversation he had with Puddin mother and Tashione said now that's a shame. Tony sat down on the chair and pulled out the envelopes and seen that one had her parents name on it. He reached Tashione one and he read his. They both were crying by the time they got done. Tony got himself together and called the boys name so they could go home. Back at the house, Tony told the boys that he had a letter to read them from mommy. Tony looked at his sons and when Mickey looked back at him, Tony just couldn't do it and started crying. Tashione got the letter from Tony and read the boys what their mommy had wrote them. Junior asked Tashione was she going to be their mommy now? Tashione picked him up and said yes I can be your mommy now. How about you and me go get some ice cream. Yeah I would like that very much. Mean while in the boys room Tony was trying to deal with his son Mickey about his mother's death. I want my mommy now! She's not dead! You are just saying that to get me and my brother to stay with you and that bitch. Hold up Mickey, I have told you about cursing and you have no choice but to stay with us. Your mommy went to heaven and she is going to be watching over us all now. Mickey tried to run out the room but his father grabbed him and held him in his arms. Mickey was still yelling and cursing. Tashione came out the kitchen and hugged Mickey as well. All he could do now was hit her on her back asking for his mommy. Tashione just held him while he cried and then it turned into sobs. Tashione looked at Mickey and said come here let me read you something that your mother wrote to you. She started reading the letter to him, but Mickey had so much mixed emotions. He didn't know whether to hate his mother for leaving him or keep loving her. After she was done reading the letter, Mickey apologized for his behavior and how he was treating her. Tashione told Mickey that she understand how he feels and didn't blame him for it. Do you want some ice cream now? I guess so. Tony fixed his son some and watched how Tashione handled his kids and felt nothing but love for her. Once the funeral was over Mickey changed all together; he started calling Tashione mommy now and things was going great. Tashione still couldn't believe that Brian came to the funeral and wasn't in jail like he was supposing too. Tashione knew then that Puddin had taken the rap for him and didn't know she would get that much time. Tashione told Tony that Brian looked very familiar to her, but couldn't place his face. Things were getting back to normal and the boys didn't think about their mother's death as much. The telephone rung and when Tashione picked up a male voice said you are next bitch and hung up. Tashione just hung up and went to take her shower since the boys were in the bed for the night. By the time, she got out and dresses the phone rung again and it was the same voice saying I'm coming for you soon bitch. (Click) Tashione was really getting scared now and Tony still wasn't home yet. She checked on the boys and then went to her bedroom to call Tony cell phone but got no answer. The phone rung again and this time she said "look motherfucker stop calling my house," but it was Tony this time. Hey, baby, what's wrong. I was just calling you back since you called my cell phone and I'm almost home. Tashione kept Tony on the phone till he got home. Tashione had the front door open and waiting on Tony to get out the car. Tony asked her was she okay and she just started crying; saying someone keeps calling making threats to me. Tony got the phone and called the police to report it and someone will there shortly. Tashione went to locking all windows and even went back to check on the boys too. The doorbell rung and she jumped a little, Tony open the door and it was a police officer standing there like he really didn't give a fuck. Tony invited him in and he got right down to asking questions. By the time, he was done the phone rung and the police officer answered it with a hello. The voice on the other end said can't nobody help that bitch now; I'm getting closer by the minute the past is catching up to you. (Click) The officer asked again did she have any idea who could be doing this. I'm sorry officer but I don't know who that could be or why they are even doing this to me. Well we are going to help you as much as we can, but in the mean time get your number changed and make sure it's non public. Once the police officers left, the woman told her partner that we got to help her. She got two small children at home and my heart goes out to her because I got children of my own. Let's go back to the station to get our equipment so we can bug her phone and put some cameras around her house as well. Tashione was a nervous wreck and begun to cry on Tony shoulders. An hour later went by before the police officers were back with bags on their shoulders. They explained what they were doing to the house and hope it didn't cause any problems for them. Tony told them to do what ever it took to help protect his family. Once they had the phone bugged, all they needed was the man to call again. Which he did with the same message "you are going to die bitch." The woman officer told Tashione to keep him talking longer on the phone, so she did by asking him why are you doing this to me? He told her, no this will not work and hung up the phone up. The police couldn't get a trace but they had the phone bugged so maybe they will next time. They gave them their cards and left. Tony told Tashione to come on so they could go to bed. He took a shower and Tashione was lying in the bed waiting for Tony to get out of the shower. When he got out, he got right in the bed and held her in his arms till she fell asleep. Tony was now wondering who this sick mother fucker was and why he's out to get his future wife. Tony finally closed his eyes and went to sleep.

CHAPTER 14

(Present) When Tashione moved she almost fell off Derrick lap and he caught her. Tashione had a death grip on his arm and luckily he had a blanket over it, because Tashione nails was biting in. Derrick said Tashione I got you baby and she loosened up her grip. I apologize for that and hope I didn't break the skin. Derrick picked her back up and held her in his arms saying, no you didn't break the skin. I know your back is hurting from sleeping like that. And you are more than welcome to go get in my spare bed upstairs. No, I'm okay as long as I have you in my arms. Tashione laughed and said okay but I warned you. He lifted her face so he could give her a kiss. It was a rather slow passionate kiss that left her breathless. Tashione was the first to break the kiss, then she looked at Derrick and said come on let's go to my bedroom. Derrick stop her by saying it's okay Tashione. Derrick I really want this to happen between us. I feel something I haven't felt in a long time; and plus you don't know shit about me and I don't know nothing about you. Tashione got up and pulled him by the hand and this time he followed. While going up the stairs they heard the glass break and Derrick took off to go see where it came from. By the time, Keith made it down the stairs he found Derrick in the living room. Someone had thrown a brick and had a picture tape to it with the word bitch on it. Derrick showed Tashione the picture and it was of her, Tony and the boys. That tore a scream from her and Derrick asked what does it mean? She was crying to bad to even get the words over the lump in her throat. Tashione finally was able to talk and she told Derrick and Keith about the people in the picture. Derrick asked where they are now. They were killed several years ago. He told Tashione that he had to call the percent to get someone over here. I need to go check on Soul any way. When Tashione opened the door Soul was sound asleep, so she closed the door back. Tashione went back down stairs to sit and talk with Keith and Derrick. There was a knock at the door and when Derrick opened the door; there was officer in uniform greeting him. They all sat down and she listen to Derrick take charged of things. Keith was putting up a wooded board up over the window while they were talking about what happen. Derrick told the officer that was there to take the report. That he had a suspect in mind, but he wasn't sure if it was the same person. Tashione looked at him like he was crazy, she knew it was Raul and she wanted him behind bars. The officer told them that he had all the information that he needed and he got up to leave. Once Derrick closed the door, Tashione went off on him. What the hell you mean you aren't sure about the suspect, you, and I both know that it's Raul who is doing this to me. Sit down for a minute and just hear me out. Now how long have you known Raul? This is bullshit Derrick. No because the person who threw the brick through the window had to know you from your past. That statement made Tashione think and agree with him. We got to talk more about this later but right now can we finish what you started. Tashione held out her hand and they went back to her room. Keith just watched and laughed to himself before he got back in the bed with Soul. When Tashione open the door she screamed, and Derrick pushed her aside pulling out his gun. Once things was clear he told Tashione to come in, when she got half way in the room, Soul came running. What the fuck is wrong! Tashione curtain around her bed had been slashed and someone cut her mattress up. Soul told them to look on the wall and that's where they seen "Bitch you will die soon." Derrick told Tashione and Soul that they will go to his house till they solved this case. Derrick told Soul to go pack some clothes now and she left right away. Tashione on the other hand was in shock and wasn't moving or saying a word. Derrick grabbed her, calling her name several times and still no response. He begins to shake her and when he slapped her, she came back to reality. Derrick pulled her in his arms while she cried on his shoulder, baby listen I'm taking you to my house and need you to pack some clothes. Tashione just agreed to what he said. Once they had their stuff packed up and ready to leave, Derrick told Tashione to put the alarm on the house. Keith told them he would follow them. Once they were going down the road Soul fell asleep and Tashione was nodding on his shoulder. By the time, they got to Derrick house he unlocked the door and cut the lights on. He went back to the car to wake the ladies up and help with the bags. He showed Soul to his guest bedroom. He told Tashione she can use the other room across from his. Tashione told Derrick thank you and gave him a kiss before retiring to bed. Derrick looked at his watch and said damn it's almost 1:00 a.m. and I got to get up at 6:00 am . Keith was knocking on the door saying man we got to get some sleep and I can't make it to my house can I crash here for the night. You know you can and told him where Soul was at. Thanks man I owe you big time. He locked up and went to his room and laid across the bed and dozed right off. Tashione was trying to sleep but couldn't and got up and went and got in the bed with Derrick. Derrick alarm clock went off and he tried to stop it before it woke up Tashione. Tashione asked Derrick what time is it. It's 6:00 a.m. and you need to go back to sleep. I will see you in a couple of hours. She rolled back over and went to sleep, because she felt safe and her body was emotionally and physical drained. Derrick got in the shower and got dress for work. He looked at Tashione sleeping body and couldn't believe how he brought another woman in his home after what happen to him before. However, looking at Tashione sleep so peaceful, he felt drawn to her and it didn't seem so bad of an idea now. Derrick first love had hurt him so bad, he wouldn't allow another woman to get close to him again. Derrick had found his fiancée in bed with another woman. He had got off from work early to spend time with his soon to be wife, and walked in on her and girlfriend doing the 69. What the hell is going on? His fiancée told him to come and join them. Derrick told her she was a sick bitch and for both of them to get out of his house. He walked over to Tashione and kissed her before he left for work and she only mumble the words I love you. He was shocked and stunned at the same time; he couldn't believe she said that to him. Derrick decided to go ahead and leave and called out for Keith to come on. They drove separate cars because they both got off at different times. Keith went to clock in and then he went to Derrick office to talk about what they are going to do about Tashione and Soul. Listen man I can take Soul to my house because I am really feeling her and want more from her. She got a mouth on her, but all she need is a good man to love her. I really can't say how I feel about Tashione because I won't let myself feel love again. Man you can't be serous about that. Oh, I am Keith, and I owe all this shit to my ex. I would ask you about it but it's none of my business. I will say this much to you don't let the past ruin your life now. I hear what you is saying but it's so hard for me to get over the hurt she caused me. So what do you want to do about Raul? I don't think he had anything to do with it. I think someone is using him as a throw off. I don't agree with that at all and I feel he has something to do with it. He may not be the one pulling the damn trigger but he know who is and I'm going to be there to bust his ass. Derrick has never heard Keith talk like that and he was really worried since he was falling for Soul. Keith asked Derrick do he want to bring Raul ass back in for questions. No but I need to talk to Tashione about her husband death. Keith had his doubts but went along with it anyway. Keith and Derrick went to a chalk board and started writing information down. All the shit still points at Raul; Keith kept saying I told you so man. No Keith; you are wrong about this one. How about we get all the information on Tashione husband death first and see where this leads us. I still think you are wrong about this said Keith. Derrick got on the computer to pull up a case number on Tashione husband death. When he got the case number and pulled it up on his computer his mouth dropped open. Keith came around to see what had come up. Oh my god man, this is some fucked up shit. Who ever done that is a sick mother fucker to kill her husband and two little boys. See man I told you this is someone else and they are using Raul as a cover up. Okay I'm feeling you on this but what now? We go and talk to the Captain and see if he will make you my partner. They went to talk to the Captain and he didn't have a problem with them working together on this case. Keith told Derrick that Tashione shot someone who was at her house right. Yeah but what does that have to do with anything. Well who ever she shot may be our suspect. Get a check list from the hospital to see if anybody came there with a bullet wound. I will call Tashione to let her know that we will be coming there to ask her a few questions. Once both of them finish doing what they said; they headed out for Derrick house. Keith cell phone rung and it was Soul on the phone. He asked her was everything okay and she said yes. Soul told him that she miss him and can't wait to see him, well I miss you too and will be there in a few minutes. Okay baby, I will see you then. (Click) Soul was all smiles and Tashione said well look at you! Tashione asked Soul was she hungry? Not for food and started laughing. Tashione got to looking through Derrick cabinets and refrigerator to find it only had frozen dinners. How in the hell does a man live off this shit. Girls stop tripping and put two of them in the oven. We can always go to the store later on since we don't have a car here to drive. Tashione dial Derrick cell phone to ask him to bring her car to her. He was in a shitty mood and took it out on her. How about I bring you the car later. Well I really need to get some food in your house if we are going to stay here. I said it will be later. (Click) Tashione looked at the phone and said damn what got him pissed off? Derrick knew he had little to eat at his place and they stop at her house so Keith could drive her car back to his place. Derrick called back to his house and told Tashione that they will be shortly with her car. (Click) Look, the fellows will be here with my car soon and then I am going home. Soul looked at her liked she was crazy and got mad because now she felt like Tashione was playing with her life. What is up with you girl? Nothing is up but I'm going back home. I don't need this bullshit from Derrick. I can protect myself and I don't need him for shit. Tashione went to the room where she had her clothes at and started flinging shit in her bag. Soul watched her friend for a few minutes and said girl you is crazy to be playing with your life like that. Look, you can stay but I'm out. When Derrick and Keith pulled up they heard the two women arguing about something and they went in. Soul told Derrick that Tashione was leaving to go back home. Are you fucking crazy or what? I can take care of myself! I don't need you or the bullshit. Who have my keys to my car? Nobody said anything at first, and then Derrick grabbed Tashione by her arm to lead her to his bedroom. Look Derrick you seem to have a problem with me being here so I am going to go back to my own house. Tashione will you listen to me for a minute. You want to know what is wrong with me! Well I'm falling in love with you and I'm fighting it really hard. Tashione was speechless and didn't know what to say. She walked up to him and laid her hand on his arm to let him know it was okay to feel that way. Derrick you need to talk to me because I don't understand what or why you are fighting your feelings for me. He sat on the bed and asked her too sit as well. I was engaged one time to a lady who was my high school sweetheart and one day I came home from work and caught her in bed with another woman. Do you know she had the fucking nerve to ask me to join them? What did you do then? I told her I wanted her gone by the time I got back home. Tashione lift Derrick head up and told him I'm not her and please don't make me pay for her mistake either. I am falling in love with you to and I'm scared as hell because everybody that I ever loved end up getting killed. I don't want that to happen to you. Derrick looked at her and promises to always protect her with his life. Tashione asked him was he hungry? Yeah I could eat a little something. They left and went to the kitchen to find all kinds of things to make sandwiches with. I see you two are already eating up everything. Derrick smiled at her and started to make him a sandwich to eat. After they ate lunch, Keith and Soul went in the bedroom and Derrick asked Tashione a couple of question about her marriage to Tony. Once he had some of his answers, he called Keith name so they could get back to the percent. Tashione asked him what time will he be getting home and he said around six or seven tonight. Don't worry about cooking anything because I plan on taking you out to dinner. Oh, Derrick you don't have to but that would be nice. Keith kissed Soul and told her he will be here to get her when he got off from work. I will be here waiting for you. Derrick gave Tashione a spare key to his house and then they left. When they got back to the percent the Captain called them in and told them it was a go; but Keith had to turn in his old badge for the new badge. Keith was smiling so hard and Derrick said alright then partner and hit him on his back. Derrick and Keith had just became partners and a new friendship was forming. Tashione wanted to go shopping for some food but Soul said she was tired and wanted to take a nap. Tashione notice the changes in her and asked was she okay. Soul looked at her friend and said I'm pregnant. Tashione was happy for her and was talking about what all she was going to do for her god child. Soul wasn't to thrill about it. Have you made a Doctor's appointment yet? Yes and its tomorrow afternoon so will you go with me. You know I will be there for you, have you told Keith yet? Hell no and I don't even know how to tell him. Souls asked her not say a word about this till she talks to Keith herself. Soul went to her room and lay across the bed and started crying. Tashione sat on the couch and was listening to the radio. A song came on that reminded her of Tony and she realized that she still missed him a lot. She felt cheated because they just got to spend their life as a family till that dreadful night. Tashione let the tears fall and then she called Cinnamon. When she answered the phone and heard Tashione voice she was happy as hell. They caught up on everything and everybody. When Cinnamon told Tashione that

Licet had a baby boy and named him Tony after her brother. Tashione was happy but it still hurt like hell. Can I ask you something Cinnamon? Sure baby. Will it ever get easy for me to live without Tony and the boys? Yes baby, only time will heal your pain and broken heart. It's getting late and I know you got to work in the morning so I'm going to let you go, I love you. Tashione please don't take so long in calling me because you are still family and I love you too. (Click) Tashione got on her knees to say a prayer and asked God to take the empty feeling away and to put someone in her life to help fill the void. When she got up and took her shower, she went to Derrick bed and fell asleep peaceful for the first time in many nights. Derrick and Keith came in the house to find it quiet as hell and Derrick got scared and ran to his room to see if Tashione was still there. He opens the door to find her lying in his bed sleeping like a baby. He couldn't figure out how he ended up with a beautiful woman in his life again. He closed the door and told Keith that she was still here and if he wanted to, he could spend the night with Soul. Keith went in the room that Soul was in and gave her a kiss to wake her up. She rolled over with a smile on her face and pulled him down for a kiss. She told him that she needed to talk to him and it was very important. He sat up and she told him that she might be pregnant by her ex. Keith got up off the bed and asked her what are you telling me. Keith me and Vern have broke up and I will tell him once I find out for sure that I'm pregnant, but we will not be getting back together. Keith felt the stress lift up off him and he got back in the bed to hold her while she cried. Derrick went back to his room and took a shower and got in the bed beside Tashione and wrapped his arm around her. The next morning Tashione was drinking a cup of coffee when Derrick and Keith came in the kitchen saying Good morning. Soul came in next and she look liked shit and Tashione knew but didn't know if Keith did. Girl you look rough did Keith keep you awake all night. Girl I told him last night and I been up sick all morning. Keith asked Soul would she mind staying at his place. Soul looked at Tashione and said I think I should stay with her till this shit is over. Girl listen we can spend all day together but when the guys get off you go with Keith and I stay with Derrick okay. Soul leaped for joy and gave her friend a kiss and said oh my god I'm going to be sick and ran for the bathroom. They all laughed at her. Once she came out of the bathroom Keith asked was she okay. Yes; I'm fine but this morning sickness I can do without. They got in Keith car and pulled off, leaving Tashione and Derrick alone at the house. Derrick asked did she want a glass of wine. Yes, that would be fine. Do you mind if I cut on some music. Go right ahead and sit by the fireplace so we both will be comfortable. When Derrick came out he reached Tashione a glass and he sat right next to her. Tashione took a sip before she asked him how his day was. It was pretty laid back today, not much going on at the office. Derrick have you found out any more about what's going on? Look Tashione I really don't want you to worry yourself about it okay. Do you want to dance? Tashione told him that she hasn't dance in so long and I will dance like I have two left feet. Well let's just see what you working with woman. Derrick helped her up and pulled her in his arms and moved to the beat of the music. In the middle of dancing, Derrick told Tashione that he wanted to make love to her. She froze in his arms and looked up with tears in her eyes. Tashione what is wrong baby? Oh nothing, I have been very sensitive lately, and I feel like I'm on a roller coaster. Before she could finish her sentence, Derrick had her hand on his dick to show her what effects she have on him. Did I do that!! They both started laughing. Tashione caressed his dick in his pants and heard Derrick moan softly. I have an idea Derrick and pulled him toward the swimming pool. What you want to make love in the water? No but I do want to be in the pool so she pushed him in. Tashione started undressing and dived in the pool. When she came up, she was in front of Derrick and pulled him in for a kiss. Derrick broke the kiss and went for her nipples and gently sucked the water off. Tashione leaned her head back and offered him the other one. Derrick lifts her up to the edge of the pool and spread her legs open. He first started licking and sucking on her toes. Not knowing that it was her Hot Spot. Then he slowly worked his way up to her thighs leaving his passion marks right behind his licks and sucks. He stopped to see if it was okay to go on and when she didn't stop him, he continue on doing his thing. He spread her pussy lips apart till her clitoris was showing and then wrapped his lips around it. Oh, god that feels so good to me. Derrick was good at eating pussy and it all showed by the way Tashione was moving her hips to his movement. She was pulling his head in closer like he could get all up in it. She was grinding her hips to meet the building climax that every woman gets when he is on the right spot. Derrick then stuck his fingers in her pussy gradually, then he was stroking her. Oh, yes baby, faster please! Oh yeah, right there. Oh, shit I'm about to cum and she did all over his fingers. He pulled it out and sucked all her juices off then winked his eye at her. He then went down to clean the mess he made there and doing a little humming on the clit, which brought her another moan and her body bowing some. Tashione thought he was finish and tried to get up. Where do you think you are going? I'm not done with your ass yet! Tashione loved to hear a man use a little bass in their voice and sat back down by the pool. Derrick laid her back and spread her legs again. The next thing she felt was his finger going in her ass, she flinched some. Try to relax baby and enjoy this new pleasure I'm about to give you. You can bet you ass she did just that. Derrick had her begging him to stop but he wanted her to feel what it was like to cum both ways. Her body begins to tremble and shake so much that when she nut, she let a big ass scream fall off her lips. Derrick came out of the pool dripping water all over Tashione who was now squealing. Tashione held her hand up and Derrick pulled her up. She wrapped her arms around Derrick neck and begun to tongue his ass down. He carried her all the way to his bedroom and sat her down on the bed; while he went to run some water in the shower. They took turns washing each other till it later turned into a caressing game. Tashione rinsed the soap off and got out, leaving a puzzled Derrick behind. Since I know you can suck and finger pussy let's see how good you can fuck it. Derrick got out the shower so fast that he almost fell. She lies on the bed and he crawls over her real slow like he is stalking his prey. He puts her arms over her head, spread her legs with his knees, and glides his dick home. He moves slowly at first to let her get used to his thickness. My god you are thick! Has anybody ever told you that? He laughed and said am I hurting you? No, but I do have to adjust to your thickness. Once he had her wet enough she was fine and moving to meet his thrusts. She wraps her legs around him; and Derrick was like damn woman you feel so good! I want the doggy style now and they changed position. He palms her ass and slides his dick in her hot wet pussy hard and making Tashione moans some. I need for you to go fast and hard okay. Derrick hated for a woman to tell him how to make love to her, but he didn't say anything to her. He just gave it to her the way she wanted it. When it was time for her to cum he slowed it down letting her pussy muscles tighten up around his dick. Derrick seen that she nutted and smacked her ass to get her attention. Oh yes I been a bad girl. (Whack) I promise to be good. (Whack) oh fuck this pussy. She had one hand on the headboard and the other one playing with her clit. It was feeling so good to her she started acting like a mad woman and Derrick was loving every minute of it. Derrick was the type of man who let his woman get off first, then he busts his nut. I'm about to cum baby are you ready? He went faster and harder and they both end up cumin together. He fell on top of her and she told him to get his big ass off her, I can't breath. When he moved she just laugh and got in between his arms so he could hold her. Tashione gave him a kiss and said I need a nap. That's right you fuck this pussy so well that I need a nap, and they both dozed off. The telephone started ringing. Derrick answered and when he heard fire, he jumped straight up and said be right there. (Click) He tapped Tashione shoulder and told her someone tried to burn her house down. She jumps up and put on a sweat suit he had reached her. Once they arrived, the fire department told her that they caught it just in time; we got a call from the neighbors. Det. Green asked where the neighbors are now. He was told that they were near the truck. He went straight for them to ask them a few questions. When he reached them he spoke and went right for main question, did you see the person who did this? No, we didn't see their faces because they had on masks and black clothes on. We did make our presence known to them and that's why we were able to call the Fire Department in time. Tashione thanked the old couple and started to cry. Derrick pulled her in his arms and told her it will be okay. She looked up at him and said when! I am so sick of this mother fucker messing with my life; I have lost so much behind this person. I know you are upset, but I promise I will get this bastard soon. They got in the car and headed for his house. Once inside Derrick asked Tashione to sit down for a minute. I need to know what happen to you in your past. She was crying now and told him that she was in a gang and her first boyfriend had taught her how to fire a gun. What happen to him? She wiped her eyes and said he took a bullet for me and died later. I didn't know baby, I'm sorry. One of the other gang members was in love with me and didn't want me with nobody else but him; and I didn't feel the same way about him. He shot my boyfriend and I shot and killed him. Derrick was looking at her like wow, I can't believe you went through all that at a young age. I was the black sheep in my family and always stayed in trouble. The only way I could get my education was to move south. Before you even asked, my birth mother lived there. He started laughing and said come on so we can get some sleep. I wonder how things are going with Soul and Keith. I bet she is in his arms sleeping, which you are about to be in mines. He won't let anything happen to her so stop worrying yourself okay. Derrick was up before her so he started making breakfast. He had this gut feeling that who ever this person is was out on a revenge binge. There was still some unanswered questions but Derrick decide to let it go for now. Tashione comes in the kitchen and fixed her a cup of coffee and kiss Derrick on the top of his head before sitting down. Derrick was in a deep thought and didn't hear Tashione calling out his name. She yelled and he jumped. What baby. You are a thousand miles from here, are you okay? Yes just thinking about some things that's all. I'm ready for breakfast now. Well what would you like for me to cook? He pulled her in front of him and lifts her up on the table. He opens her robe and said you don't have anything on. I always sleep nude, is it a problem for you? Oh hell no! In addition, he begins to caress her nipples till they were rock hard. She lean her head back some and moan his name out. Derrick get up and strip his pants and shoes off, then gets on the table with Tashione. I hope it will hold the both of us. They got in the 69 position and ate off each other till they had their fill. Soul and Keith had walked in on them, and when Keith was about to say something Soul said no and pull him out toward the living room. Tashione sees them but refused to get up off the dick. When they were done Tashione told Derrick that Keith and Soul are here, and he freak out. He was pulling on his pants and fussing at her because she should have told him. Oh, stop being a baby, so what if they saw us doing each other. I'm sure Keith is doing it himself. Tashione walked in the living with Derrick right behind her. Soul asked how was breakfast? And started laughing while Keith puts his head down. Girl you know I'm a strong believer in having proteins in my diet, and the girls cracked up. Keith could not help himself and he laugh too, while Derrick was mad as hell. They kissed the girls and left for work. Soul was smiling and told Tashione that Keith was shocked as hell to see you'll do it on the table. I told Derrick his ass is in for a lot more surprises. I just couldn't stop myself it was feeling to good. Soul said well I'm going to my old room and take a nap. Long night! Yes and no it was not Keith it was me being sick as hell. Well you go ahead and I can take me a shower and do the same.

CHAPTER 15

(Past) Tashione heard someone calling her name, but didn't want to move. Then she felt someone jumping on the bed, saying open your eyes. When she did, it was junior saying daddy got a surprise for you? Mommy he won't let me see it until you get up, so come on please. She told junior to leave the room so she could put some clothes on. When the door closed she put on her pj's and told junior to come on. She picked him up and laid him on the bed tickling him and Mickey came in to saying Ma! Daddy want you so please come on because I'm hungry. Tell daddy I'm coming already and I have to put my robe on. She grabbed junior and carried him downstairs to see what the fuss was about. Junior wanted down so she put him down and he ran to the kitchen. When she got there her favorite men was standing at the table waiting on her with big smiles on their faces. Baby what is going on? Just have a seat please and she does as told. All three of them got on one knee and asked her to marry them. Tashione seen the ring in Tony hand and the boys had a rose in theirs. She started crying saying Yes I will marry you'll and they all charged her for some love. Mickey had become very protective of her since his mother died. Tashione was loving it because she didn't have kids of her own and it wasn't from lack of trying either. Okay guys enough of hugs and feed me some breakfast. Mickey asked what do you want mama? Can I please have my specialty, which was a bowl of Fruity Pebbles Cereal? Once they were all done eating and the dishes clean back up, Tashione went to take a shower. Tony told the boys that we are going to grandma's house to tell everybody. They all loaded up in the car and before they got to Bklyn, they had to stop and get the boys something from McDonalds. Tashione told Tony she loved him and can't wait to spend the rest of her life with him and the boys. While waiting on the food she kept looking at her ring like it was all a dream and would wake up real soon. Baby what ever happen to my first ring you gave me? Tony said baby look at the ring real good. She took the ring off and checked it out and said oh my god it's my ring with a bigger diamond. That ring was meant for just you, he turned to pay for the food and handed the boys the bag. Okay now tell me this why are the boys being extra good? I know you promise them something so what is it. I have to give them twenty dollars for not spoiling your day. Tashione turned around and said boys I will give you ten more dollars if you act the way you normally do. The boys bust out laughing and Tony did too. Once they arrived at Cinnamon house the boys took off, then came back holding their hands out. Tony gave them their money, but Tashione said later so you won't spend it all up today. They asked could they go to the game room to play and Tony said okay. Tony called out for his ma to hurry up and when she did, the boys told her that they asked Tashione to marry them. Tony father came out the room with his hair all messed up and Cinnamon looked embarrassed. Cinnamon asked what are you'll looking at. Look at you two; his hair messed up and your dress is caught in your panties. Tashione started laughing so hard that tears were rolling down her face. Tony father walked over to him and said I'm very proud of you son and gave him a hug. Cinnamon said let's celebrate tonight and you'll can stay here if you like. Licet came in and said ma I'm sick. That's what happens when you get pregnant. What! Who the fuck is the father asked by both father and brother. Licet told them none of their business and plus I'm grown so chill out. Tashione said I'm going to be an auntie. Licet said yes and I want to be in the wedding belly and all. How! Never mind you over heard us talking. Mickey came in with his brother and when Tashione seen them, she yelled oh my god. Granddad Tony was the first to ask what happen. When Mickey told them, they got into a fight with some of the boys at the game room. Tony asked did they kick ass. Mickey looked and said Hell yeah! Tashione yelled Mickey! he said well ma. Cinnamon told them to go gets cleaned up. Tony walked up to Tashione and hugged her saying you know I have been in love with you since the beginning of us meeting. I love you to baby, but we need to let my folks know about us getting married too. Mickey walked in saying god do you'll ever get tired of doing the nasty and junior laughed. After eating dinner with Tony family it was time to go home the boys were played out. They both carried the boys and put them to bed after getting her good night kiss from them. Tashione was in their bedroom undressing, and then she ran a hand across her belly asking God to bless her with a child. Tony was watching her from the door way and knew how bad she wanted one. Once Tony came in the room, Tashione jumped and started putting on her gown. They got in bed and the phone rung and Tony answered it. No one said anything, but Tony heard the person breathing and just hung up. Tashione asked who it was and Tony said whoever it was had the wrong number. Tony pulled Tashione in his arm and asked her are you okay. She turned in his arms to face him and said yeah, but I know it was that person again and I want you to stop lying to me. Tony fell asleep while Tashione just stared at the ceiling till she dozed off. The alarm was going off and Tony hit the snooze button. Tashione got on up and wash her face and brushed her teeth. She went to the kitchen to start breakfast and once it was done, she called for them to come eat. They all came in half ass sleep and she knew no one washed their faces or brushed their teeth. While they were eating, she made the beds up and had their clothes laid out for school. Once breakfast was over the boys was ready to put their clothes on and Tony got back in bed. Tashione knew where her future husband was so she went to the bedroom and snatched the covers back. Get you ass out of bed so you can get ready for work. Tony butt was getting fat and Tashione called him tub boat. Tony jumped up and grabbed Tashione to tickle her and the boys came in, one saying get him mommy, and the other said get her daddy. Tashione finally said okay, I give. Tony got up and said I love you so much and kissed her, while the boys were saying not the nasty. Tony pulled away and said got to get ready for work and will see you when I get home. Now remember don't come home till it's almost time for me to get here as well. Tashione got dressed and the boys loaded in the car. Here comes Tony out the house with just his pants on, so Tashione rolled the window down and said what is it baby? I called in and told my boss what is going on and he gave me the day off so I can go with you to your parents' house. When they got there Junior went to yelling that Mickey hit him, and grandpa told them to come here right now. Listen to me I will not have you hitting on your brother and you need to get tuff and stop acting like a baby. Papa doesn't tell him that cause look where that comment got me. Tony spoke to everyone and took a seat right next to Tashione dad. Tashione went to everybody rooms to get them so they could hear what was being said. Once everybody was in the living room Tony asked Tashione parents for her hand in marriage. Rosa was happy but her father yelled out Hell No! Tony asked him could they speak in private and Tashione told her father to be nice. Divine took the boys to his room so they could play the game and everybody else just looked crazy. Back in the bedroom, it was quiet at first, and then all of a sudden they heard a bunch of arguing. Rosa and Tashione took off for the room and then they heard something fall and break. They thought Papa had jumped on Tony; but Papa knocked over Rosa floor mirror and it shattered.

CHAPTER 16

(Present) When Tashione got up, she saw that Soul was sitting by the pool, all quiet. Tashione was really worried about her because Soul had finally found happiness with Keith and she might lose it because she is pregnant. Hey girl, it's almost time to go for your Doctor appointment is you ready? Yes I guess, but I'm scared that I will lose Keith. Later on in the Doctor office Soul was very quiet and in deep thought that she did not hear her name being called. Tashione tapped her on the arm and they got up and went to meet the nurse. In the room, Soul had to pee in a cup and watch while the test shows her that she Is indeed pregnant. Tashione was happy but Soul wasn't at all. The nurse said it's positive and we will set your appointment with prenatal, but here are some vitamins for you to take to help make sure the Baby is healthy. Soul didn't react till they got in the Car to burst out crying. Tashione pulled her best Friend to her arms to hug her for support. You know You got to tell the birth father. Soul Pulled back and to look at Tashione and said I don't Know how to tell Vernthat I'm pregnant. What about my relationship with Keith; would he be willing to raise this child as his? Girl stop this shit right now! You know damn well that Keith is a good man. I'm sure he would stay with you, so give him the choice to make without you making it for him. Back at Derrick house the telephone begin to ring and Soul jumped. Tashione answered it and it was Keith wanting to talk to Soul. Hold on Keith here she is now; Tashione reached her the phone in addition, whispered for her to tell him. Tashione started to think about if she would ever have children of her own; which she so badly wanted. Soul was off the phone with Keith and told Tashione that she was going to call the father to let him know that she is Pregnant. She dials his number and he picks up on second ring. Hello Vern this is Soul, I am calling to let you know that I'm pregnant with your child. Soul heard the telephone drop and then Vern saying Oh Hell no! I'm not ready to be a father and he was willing togive her the money to have an abortion before hanging up. Once Soul told Tashione what Vern said she was pissed! Well what did Keith say?

I just told him that I have something important to talk to him about. Meanwhile back at the police station Derrick was pulling all kinds of information up on Tashione that was shocking to him. He came to a File that was sealed so he called a buddy of his to get access to. Derrick could not believe all the shit that Tashione was in while she was in New York. Keith walked in and asked what's up? Man check this shit out. Keith is now reading and could not believe his eyes. Damn man! Who would have ever known that she was capable of killing somebody. Derrick said look here man; she was found not Guilty because the person had raped her. They made her leave the state of New York and never to return to live there. Are you telling me that was a part of her stipulations? It sure was and I'm going to make copies of these files. Derrick asked Keith would he mind just picking Soul up and just bounce therefore, I can talk to Tashione about this. Sure man I can do that. Derrick called Tashione and told her not to cook a big meal because it was just them and they could order take out. That would be fine and I will see you when you get here and she hung up the phone. When the men got off from work and got in their cars Keith tried to call Soul but got no answer on her cell phone. Derrick was in deep thought about how he was going to bring up her Juveniles record. Which showed where she shot and killed someone, but by her being a minor the file was just wrapped up and sealed. He knew someone big or very important pulled some strings to help her out. While pulling up in the yard Tashione was standing on the porch waiting for Derrick to get out. Keith was pulling up right behind him when he seen the hesitation on Derrick side, but he walked on to Tashione and kissed and hugged her before entering his house. Soul was in the guest room steady crying; she couldn't pull herself together before Keith got there. Keith knocked on the door and Soul told him to come in. Keith saw how distraught she was and rushed to her side asking what is wrong baby? He thought she had another scare. Keith grabbed her in his arms and said everything is going to be okay. Keith picked her up and walked right pass Tashione and Derrick without saying a word. Derrick looked at Tashione in addition, she told him I will explain it to you later. So how was your day baby? It was um very interesting for a change. How so she asked. He pulled her by the hand to lead her to the conch. He was stalling for time but Tashione seen that he had something to asked her. He finally came out with a question about her past. Tashione had a look on her face like "oh Shit." Derrick notice it as well, but he did not let up. How do you know, but thought better of it because he is a Detective. Tashione said okay what you want to know about it. What ever you have to tell me will help. Well I was going with a guy name Sha at the time. Sha, me and Boo was all in the same gang together, but Boo liked me as well and I didn't like him like that. He would always flirt or push up on when Sha was not around. One day Sha and Boo got into it and Sha beat Boo ass. Of course he was embarrassed and told Sha he would get him for that. A couple of weeks went by and we didn't see Boo till the night he shot and killed Sha and I shot him in the chest. Derrick asked her how she learned to shoot a gun? Sha taught me very well, he wanted to make sure I could protect myself if I was ever alone. When I got good enough he gave me a short hand 9mm as a present. He also told me that if I pull my gun on somebody to shoot them to kill, because if I didn't killed them they would come back for me. Derrick asked what Boo real name was. Bobby Moore why do you ask. Derrick told her it could be a family member getting revenge on you. Tashione never thought about it like that. Are you okay baby? Tashione looked up and said I'm just thinking that's all. She asked Derrick do he want a beer while she was going to get her one. Yeah I can use one right about now. Tashione came back with two beers and reached him one. Derrick took a big swallow and then he asked Tashione to tell him about the other killing, she was involved in. She looked at Derrick and said you did your homework on this didn't you. Well let's see I beat a girl named Puddin ass so bad that she had a miscarriage; but she killed herself after getting 25 years in prison in addition, her boyfriend getting off free. Do you know if she had any brothers and sisters? She does but I don't know how many. How many people have you hurt and shot? There were a lot of people and I lost count. Tashione you should have been a police officer and started laughing. Tashione was getting tired of the bullshit questions; but knew it was his job. Tell me about Jerome? Tashione told him that she was at her boyfriend Jazz house and he took my gun from me because I was getting people in our gang hurt. We was getting high and I called in an order of Chinese food; while on my way back is when I was grabbed from behind. I was beat and raped without ever knowing who did that to me for a long time. We got into some beef with Jerome gang and while they was fighting he let it slipped out that, he raped me. When I heard it, Jazz turned to look at me and I shot Jerome in his chest and unloaded my clip in him. I went to jail for a few hours and then got bonded out. When I went to court my aunt pulled some strings to get the charges dropped; but I had to leave the state of New York for good. I could visit but I could never live there again. Derrick said damn baby you went through a lot. Tashione had an expression on her face that showed pain and sorrow; but she tried to cover it up before Derrick seen it. Derrick apologizes for bringing it up and he would make it up to her later on tonight. He took another sip of beer and asked the last and finally question about her husband and step-sons. She asked him could they talk about it later because it's still painful to talk about. Derrick nods his head. Tashione look Derrick in his eyes told him that she took a sleeping pill and it's starting to work. He got up and pulled her up from the conch and leads her to the bedroom. He then undress her, put his shirt on her, and walks toward the bed and pull the covers back. He picks Tashione up and places her on the bed and tucks her in for the night gently placing a kiss to her forehead. As soon as she laid on the pillow her eyes close and she was soundly sleeping. Derrick decide to take his shower and joins Tashione in bed.

CHAPTER 17

(PAST) Tashione and Tony were getting everything together for a small wedding. Things didn't turn out that way, they had a big wedding in Glenn Clare Gardens. Both families cook the food so it was a lot of choices to choose from. Tashione had on a short champagne color dress with a long thigh split on both sides. The head piece belongs to her step-mom, it was a tiara made into a crown. Tony had on a suit that made him look damn good. He would have put you in the mind of Don Kelly. After the vows was said and the priest pronounce you are now husband and wife there was a lot of cheering. Her father walked up to her and asked for the next dance. She haven't dance with her father since she was a little girl and he told her that she will always be his baby girl. Tashione started crying and her father hugged and then released her to Tony. Gene told them that he had something for them. The music stop playing and the people stop dancing to see what Gene was about to give them. Once everybody was quiet he said a little speech that welcome Tony to his family and that he better protect his precious gem. Tony shakes his head and Gene reach him an envelope with two round trip tickets to Puerto Rico. Tashione was so excited she ran to kiss her parents saying how much she loved them. Then the music started back with Carmen Cruz the Queen of Salsa started to singing. An hour later it was time to cut the cake. Tony was acting all polite; but Tashione smears the cake in his face and laugh. She leans in and start kissing and sucking on his face and everybody cheers her on. Everything else, fell in place from there. Imani caught the bouquet and Xavier caught the garter; but threw it to Jose. People were laughing at him because Xavier was against marriage. Tony and Tashione was getting ready to leave when Mickey and Junior came running up. Tashione bent down and asked the boys to be good for their grandparents and will see them soon. They kiss their mommy and said you look beautiful. They give Tony a high –five and ran back to Cinnamon. They get in the car and now were headed for the airport to start the honeymoon. Several months later Tony sister Licet gives birth to a baby girl and asked Tashione and Tony to be God-parents. One night while Tashione was at home cooking dinner the phone started to ring. When she answered, it was the stalker cussing her out for getting married. She hangs up the phone and calls Tony name out. When he reached the kitchen she tells him what happens and begins to cry. Tony holds his wife for comfort and to let her know he will protect her. Tony dials the police station and told them what happen, and got the same result as always and he was getting Mad. Tony wanted the stalker to call back so he can Let that sick bastard know he was not scared. Two police officer shows up at the door to take a report and then Tashione begins to rant about how they are not doing their jobs. She was sick of this shit and wanted it to stop now. Once the police officer had his say about everything Tony was now pissed and ready to go to his ass. Tony walked to the door and opened it asking them to leave now. The boys hear the yelling, in addition come down to see Tashione crying. Junior asked what is wrong and Mickey yells at his father about hurting mommy. Tashione pulls away from Tony and told the boys that daddy is not hurting me. Junior asked her why is she crying then? She looked up at Tony for help and he told the boys that some man keep calling the house cussing mommy out. Mickey walks over and tells Tashione that he will help protect her and give her a kiss before telling his brother to come on. Once they were in the comfort of their bedroom Tony starts to kiss her neck and ears. Umm Tashione moans and asked Tony are you trying to distract me? Is it working baby? Tashione turns in his arms and say yes baby its working! Please don't stop. Tony gets on top and rips her nightgown open. Tashione tell Tony to take her now, and starts laughing. He put a nipple in his mouth and gently sucks on it till it's hard as a rock. He gives the other one the same amount of attention and hears Tashione moan. It starts to thunder storm outside and soon after the rain start to fall. Right when Tony was about to slide his dick in her pussy; they hear a knock at the door. Junior is crying and Mickey is yelling let us in. Tony rolls over and grunts and Tashione put on a robe. Tashione open the door and thunder booms real loud and the boys jump in the bed. Everybody is in the bed now and Tony dozed off leaving Tashione awake. The boys are twisting and turning moreover, that woke Tony up to see his wife standing by the window watching the sky light up. He wraps his arm around her waist then asks are you okay?

Yes I'm fine, I couldn't sleep that's all. Well we are going to put the boys back in their own beds. No baby we can leave them in ours and we can make pallets on the floor. Come on Tashione you know my back can't take that hard ass floor. I promise to get a lot of blankets and then give you some if you can be quiet. Tony was down for the plan now since he could get some pussy. In the morning she woke to Junior on her back and Tony legs wrapped around hers. Mickey had the whole bed to himself, if he was big, enough he would take up the whole bed length wise. Tashione shakes Tony hand and when he rolls over, he don't even wake up. She calls his name softly and he open his eyes and sees Junior on her back and starts to laugh. He got up and picked up Junior to put him back in the bed. No wonder I felt like I was about to suffocate. Mickey was now hanging off the bed; and Tashione wondered who they get their sleeping habits from. I'm going to take my shower so I can get breakfast together. In addition, you can put those blankets up for, and get our sons bathed and dress okay. He didn't answer; I mean itI'm not playing with your chunky ass. Mickey begins to yell out mommy, mommy and Tashione picks him up saying I'm here baby. Mickey told Tashione that he dream of her again going to heaven. She told him that she will never leave daddy or you and your brother. Junior is waking up asking for something to eat as usual. Okay guys take a bath in addition, breakfast will be ready when you get done. Once they got dress and ate, Tony said he needed to go to the hardware store to pick up some cherry oak wood. Tashione asked him to take the boys while she cleans up. The boys are now begging for her to come with them and they will help her clean up. Tashione agrees and went to the bedroom to get dress. While in the car, Mickey asked his daddy to cut the radio on and here this rap song that got a lot of cuss words and begins to sing along. Tashione called out Mickey name and turned it to another station. Tony is going 50 mph and is getting ready to go into a sharp curve when he realizes the brakes don't work. Tony tells everybody to buckle up. Tashione asked what is wrong? The brakes are not working and put your seatbelt on we are about to hit the curve. Tony tries to control the car but instead, the car ends up flipping several times throwing Tashione out. When she wakes up, she is sore as hell and in a hospital bed. Tashione push the button and a nurse comes in to see what was needed of her. Tashione asked for some water and then she asked for her husband and kids. Cinnamon and Rose came in the room and asked her how she feels? Where are Tony and the boys? Cinnamon shakes her head and Tashione screams out. Rose came to the bed to help Cinnamon hold her down before she hurt herself worst. Baby you have been in a coma for a week now. Rose told Tashione that she had to have surgery, because when you were thrown out of the car the windshield cut your stomach. Tashione begged them to tell her about Tony and the boys. Cinnamon told her that Tony had a piece of the motor pierce his heart and died instantly. The boy was trapped in the car and nobody could get them out before the car exploded. Tashione was in shock now and went blank. Several days later, the hospital released her so she could go home. Tashione asked her parents to take her to see the graves and they did. Tashione got on knees and just cried her heart and soul out. She gets up and go to the Mickey grave and told him she will always love and miss him and to tell his mother she tried her best. When she got to Junior grave, she told him to watch out for his daddy and brother and she love him so much. Tashione got up and turned and passed out.

CHAPTER 18

(Present) Tashione woke up to the smell of coffee, she washed her face and brush her teeth and went downstairs. Derrick was sitting at the table sipping coffee. Tashione walks in kiss his forehead and pour herself a cup. Derrick asked Tashione how she sleeps. Good and you? Derrick said not well at all, you slept like a wild animal. Oh stop damn playing I don't sleep like that and you know this. They both started laughing; then Derrick got up and looked out the window. It's going be a pretty day today and I'm stuck in the office, while you are lying up or doing what ever it is woman do. You go on to work I will be out in your yard doing some work. Ah shit, now I know you will be working because I haven't had the time to do it myself. On the other hand, I could give you a hand if I promise not claw or bite you. It took Derrick a few minutes to catch on; but when he did Tashione was already laughing at him and he joined in as well. How about I let you claw and bite me tonight when I get off from work. Now we have a plan Detective Green. Tashione went to his bedroom and pulled out some shorts and a t-shirt to do yard work; and Derrick was on his way to the office. Tashione worked on his backyard for almost three hours till she heard her stomach growl. She fixed her some lunch and chill for a few minutes thinking about all this shit and her feelings about Derrick. Tashione called Soul and talked for a few minutes about what Keith thinks about her being pregnant by someone else. Tashione told Soul to hold up a minute because she heard someone at the door. Tashione made it to the front door and found Derrick with some bags in his hand trying to open the door. Tashione helped him out and told him that he scared the shit out of her. When she made it back to the kitchen she told Soul to come over later and they could cook out; and not to worry because it was Derrick. After they put up the stuff Tashione wanted to go out and get a few things for herself in addition, wanted Derrick to drive her. While in the drug store Tashione pickedup some tampons and douche while Derrick looking all crazy. Derrick was ready to go and told Tashione okay already let's go now. I can't believe you had

me in this store for over an hour and all you got so far is tampons and
a douche in addition, couple of other items. Well baby I need all the
stuff I got and then some; but if you let me go home I would not have
to buy any of this shit. Tashione turns around and storm away leaving
Derrick standing there calling out her name. Tashione made it to the
counter and Derrick pulled out his wallet to pay for her stuff. Tashione
reached in her pocketbook and pulled out her credit card saying I can
pay for my own shit. On their way out to the car Derrick noticed the
ground wet, he bent down and smells it and said brake fluid. Derrick
got up under the car and seen the wire was cut in half.

Derrick gets up and calls Keith to come to the drug store. Once
Keith and Soul got there Derrick told him who ever is doing this knows
Tashione is staying with me because this is my car. While the girls were
talking; Tashione asked her how she is feeling and that she see a glow to
her. I take it Keith is okay about the baby. Girl Keith is happy about
it, but we will talk later. Keith told them to drive his car back to the
house, but Derrick said no for them to wait on them. Derrick called
someone to come tow his car away. After all that was done and they
were back at his house Tashione was still a little salty with Derrick and
made sure he knew. Keith noticed it as well and asked Derrick what's
wrong with the hen? Derrick told Keith that he fucked up and would
later apologize to her. Soul told Tashione that Keith wants to help her
and girl he even asked me to marry him and adopt the baby too. Oh
Soul that is great news and now I see why you have the glow. I hope
I will be the baby god-mother. Now you know better than to ask me
some crazy shit like that. Derrick told Keith that who ever did this did
the same thing to Tashione husband car. The only one that knows she
is with me is us. Derrick told Keith that he never even paid that shit
no attention and maybe that bastard has followed us. Well look man
when we get to the office we can run all the information together and
solve this shit in addition, get on with our lives. Derrick and Keith
were grilling the food and Tashione was done with the banana pudding
and Soul was done with the salad. Soul and Tashione put the salad and
plates on the table as well as the wine glasses. Soul went back in the
house to get the silverware and some napkins. They all sat around the
table to eat and make small talk till Keith notice it was almost 9:00.
Soul helped Tashione clean back up before they got ready to leave.

Once everything was done and Keith and Soul was gone; she went upstairs to take her a hot bubble bath. Derrick didn't know what to do with himself, he started for the stairs but came back down. When he finally made his mind up Tashione was laid back in the tub with her eyes closed. Derrick just watched her for several minutes looking at her and thinking why was he being so damn stubborn and just say sorry to woman that he has fell in love with.

However, Tashione open her eyes to see Derrick back. Would you care to join me? Derrick turns around and tells her no I will catch you another time and walks out closing the door behind him. Derrick goes to the kitchen and gets him a beer and goes to his bedroom to find Tashione putting on lotion. He instantly got a hard on but tried to cover it up. Derrick can you put some on my back for me? Um sure, he told her. Tashione lay across the bed and Derrick was just looking at her butt. Tashione was wondering what was taking so long and then called out his name. Derrick jumped and the lotion came out of bottle all over his hands. Once he started rubbing the lotion on her back she moans and Derrick was trying to hold it together. Derrick knew he was losing the battle and just went with the flow. While he was rubbing her back, Tashione lift up her butt to grind it on his dick. What are you doing to me woman?Tashione roll over and look Derrick in his eyes. Look Tashione; I want to make love to you so bad that it hurts. You got me feeling all kind mixed emotions and I don't know how to handle this shit. Derrick would you please stop running your pussy eaters and just fuck me already. He looked at her like she had a double head. Since you want me to fuck you then I will. And Derrick don't be gentle either because I 'm not as fragile as I look. He grabbed her ass so rough and ram his dick in her pussy so hard that she almost screamed at him; but remembered that she wanted it that way. After he was done he just got up and walked to the shower to clean himself. When he came out Tashione was still in the aftermath of being fucked real proper. He got in the bed beside her and never even touched her. Now Tashione was really getting pissed off and didn't mind telling Derrick how she felt. Oh so now you want to bitch! Hell all I did was give you what you wanted and I'm the bad guy. Get off it Tashione and take your ass to sleep. Tashione words were caught in her throat and she turned over to go to sleep. When morning came, she didn't even go down to the kitchen for breakfast or coffee. Derrick was done with his coffee and was walking out the door hoping to see Tashione before he left for work. That didn't happen so he yelled for her to get her ass down here or he was coming up whether you are dressed or not. Tashione came down asking him what he wanted from her. He looked at her and kissed his hand and blew her a kiss before walking out the door to get in Keith car. Tashione slammed the door and a mirror fell off the wall and she cursed for the mistake she just made. When Derrick and Keith got to the office he was hype up because he just knew he was about to close this case. Come on Derrick calm down man and put me on that rush you on. Derrick pulled out a chalk board to draw a chart with all these people names on it. Derrick asked Keith to do a check on all the names he had listed. Keith was like alright. Bobby Moore was decreased and have a sibling by the name Brian and Raul Moore. The next name was Carmen Lopez who was also dead in addition, her siblings were Diamond, Ricky, and Miguel. Keith yells out oh shit! I don't believe what I am Seeing. Derrick looked at Keith and said I told you So. Keith asked Derrick what do we do now? Well We can call Tashione and let her know the names To see if she knows any of them. Derrick dialed his House and got no answer and had a bad feeling that Something was wrong. He really didn't want to push It because it was still day light outside. Soul was Tied to a chair in Derrick house. Tashione was in The kitchen nervous as hell. She wanted to know Who was behind the mask talking shit to her and gotCocky as hell. She called Raul name but got no Reaction but she knew it was him. The masked manKept telling her that he knew her day would come Soon enough. He even told her that he didn't mean To kill her sons or husband. Tashione went to jumpAt him; but he pulled the gun out and pointed it atHer head. That's right bitch jump so I can blow Your head away. Tashione sat back down and let The tears fall while she came up with a plan to getThat bastard back. I wanted your ass dead so bad That it really didn't matter who got killed because itWould hurt you all the same. Go fuck yourself you Dumb mother fucker and when you do decide to killMe make sure I'm dead. That made the mask man Go real still and quiet. He walked over to her and Slaps her so hard that it split her lip. Soul heard her yelling and screaming, then the smack! The masked man grabbed her up by the hair, dragging her to the living room where Soul sat tied up.

You know What I'm going to do for you? Let's bring back old memories okay. Do you remember when and how it felt to get rape! Tashione went dead still but held herself together. Soul screams out now and he told her that if she wasn't quiet he would rape her as Well. He pointed the gun at Tashione and told her to take off her clothes. Soul was crying and trying to break herself loose, so she could help her friend. The telephone begin to ring and Tashione jumps for telephone. However, before she could reach it, he hit her in the head to knock her out. The mask man grabs her leg to pull her to the center of the room and left her there. He turns to Soul and let her know she is in no danger now. Soul couldn't tell by the voice if it was a woman or man. Tashione was moaning now and when she tried to move, her head and body hurt like hell. Soul was trying to see if her friend was okay. Tashione was leaning against a table, trying to compose herself so she could do something. It was getting dark now and the mask man said I'm going to leave a present for your new lover. When he walked up to Tashione and kicked her in the ribs. Tashione grunts in pain and double over. Tashione told the masked man to go ahead and kill her now instead of later. No Bitch! You will die when I say you die and I owe you for so much. I'm so ready to give it to you. Soul called out to the masked person and why you not going to kill me like you did the rest of my friends? He looked at her and laughed. Oh such a true friend but you are Pregnant and I don't do the babies. He turned the gun on Tashione, telling her to get up now. When she stood up she tried to go for the gun, but he was ready for her. He took a step back and pointed it right at her head but did not pull the trigger. This was making Tashione very mad because he was toying with her now. She told him to put the gun down and they can fight this out till the end. The masked person was laughing hard and he refused to let her win by simple words. He put the gun down in addition, they squared off. The phone started ringing and Soul flinch because she knew it was the guys callingto see if they was home. Soul was hoping that Keith and Derrick would show up any time. Soul begin to wonder how this person knew she was pregnant, Since she only told Tashione and Keith and Vern. Tashione caught the masked person in his face. All Of a sudden the masked person charged and she went down with him on top. She managed to get away from him and stand up straight. Right when the masked person was close enough to her, she side step him and landed a blow to the back of his head. Tashione put a real beaten on the person at first, but the table turned so fast. The masked Person beat Tashione ass so bad, that it left themask person no choice but to shoot Tashione in the leg. Then left her laying in her own blood. Soul was crying, calling out Tashione name over and over. She felt so helpless and needed help bad. Mean while Keith and Derrick was driving fast as hell to get to his house, because he knew something was wrong. Soul had her head bent down when Keith and Derrick came busting through the door. Keith seen how Soul was and yell her name out. He untied her and her legs was so weak he had to pick her up. Derrick picked up Tashione and rushed her to the hospital. When he got her there and they admitted her she was unconscious from losing so much blood. She was rushed to surgery, leaving Derrick feeling like his world was coming to an end. Derrick was losing his mind worrying aboutTashione. Two hours later the Doctor came out and told Derrick that Tashione is going to fine, but the baby has a weak heartbeat. Derrick jumped up and

approach the Doctor asking him to please repeat himself. The Doctor said you must be the father then. Derrick said yes I am, are they going to make it. Well it's too soon to say if the baby will make it because she is only three weeks. The fetus is in a very unstable stage right now. Derrick fell down on his knees to beg God to help them make it through this. Keith and Soul both tried to comfort him but the tears would not stop. Soul asked could they go in to see her if they will be quiet; he said yes but limit your visit. Keith held the door open for Derrick and Soul. Tashione was lying in the bed motionless and Soul almost fainted. Derrick went to the bed and grabbed Tashione hand kissing it; and begging her to pull through for the sake of the baby she was carrying. Derrick could not control his crying and Keith told him that he was going to take Soul home now. Oh yeah man take her home so she can get some rest as well. Soul told Derrick that she will be back up here first thing in the morning. Derrick thanked Keith but never looking away from Tashione. Derrick laid his head on the edge of the bed and prayed to God to save them. Several hours went by and the nurses came in to check her vital signs and make sure the baby was okay. The nurse told Derrick that the baby heartbeat was getting stronger by the day. As long as she, stay in the coma the baby has a good chance of making it. You need to go home and change clothes and get you something to eat as well. She left Derrick sitting in a chair now looking out the window. Around two

a.m. Tashione call out for Derrick and he reached her in a hot second, grabbing her hand to reassure her he was there. Tashione started crying and Derrick picked her up and held her. He begged her to try to open up her eyes, she tries several times before they opened. Tashione was in a lot of pain and Derrick laid her back in the bed. He told her he was going for a nurse and took off. When they came back in and Tashione was checked out, Derrick told her that she was three weeks pregnant. Honey the baby is in danger and you need your rest, but there is a lot of questions I want to ask you. Before Tashione could answer Derrick was leaving the room, but only long enough to get the nurse in the room since Tashione had her eyes open. Once the nurse checked her vital signs and told them that things are looking real good; but she still need to see her Doctor. Tashione nodded back off to sleep and Derrick called Keith and told him the good news and hung up the telephone. Derrick laid in bed with her and watched her sleep. Derrick put his hand on her stomach and could not believe he was about to be a father. He said a prayer to God for sparing their lives and joined Tashione for some much needed rest. The next morning Keith and Soul went to the hospital to find Tashione sitting up talking to Derrick. Soul rush straight to her and gave her a hug. Tashione was ready to bounce but had to wait for the doctor to release her. When the Doctor came in and asked how is my patience? I am doing fine and want to go home, so do you think you can release me today? Everybody in the room called out Tashione name. What! Damn I hate hospitals and Soul you already know this so stop fucking tripping. The Doctor said well lets check you and the baby and go from there. After he checked her out he told her that she can't go no where till the baby is out of danger. Tashione wanted to leave but her child safety was more important to her. The Doctor left the room and Derrick, Keith, and Soul came back in. Well you guys I'm stuck here till the baby is completely out of danger. Well do you want or need anything? Tashione said I'm hungry! Everybody bust out laughing and Derrick asked Keith to join him. Tashione told Soul that once she got better that she was going to do her own digging for the person that did this to her. Soul just looked at her friend and knew not to say a word because all it did was give her that extra push. Twenty minutes went by and Derrick reach her a bag of fruits and a sandwich from subway. Tashione looked at first, then she started to eat. Soul had told Keith what Tashione plans were and he was going to tell Derrick as soon as he got the chance. Tashione asked Derrick did he find out anything. Keith was trying to tell him not to say anything, but Derrick wasn't paying any attention and told Tashione everything. The plan of revenge was in motion and she couldn't wait. Soul was watching Tashione and she knew what time it was. Soul didn't agree with that thought she was having and asked the guys could she be along with Tashione. Derrick told her that he was going to the house to take a shower and be back later. Once they left Keith told Derrick what Soul had told him;and he could not believe she would put their child in danger. He started to turn around but Keith stop him; telling told him wait till she make her move then say something. Soul is the only one that know and you will have two best friends fall out. You right man so I'm going to wait, look I need to take a shower so I can get back. Soul looked at her friend sitting on the bed and asked her what was on her mind? Tashione looked up and said nothing. Soul knew her friend better than that and said I'm waiting. Look Soul I have to get them before they get me and my baby. What about the baby girl! Tashione said I have a couple of months before I even start to show signs that I'm pregnant. I can not believe what I'm hearing; have you lost your fucking mind or is this hospital doing something to your mind. What if you lose the baby because you want revenge! Soul storm out the room and told Keith what Tashione is doing. Look baby I told Derrick and he is going to watch her real close so she won't do anything stupid. He hugged her and they left to go home. Tashione understood how her friend felt, but she wanted and needed Soul to understand. Tashione felt so helpless but then the need to get revenge became her main goal. The nurse came in the room to check on her and the baby. Listen young lady you need to get some rest because the baby heart rate is dropping again.

CHAPTER 19

Tashione got comfortable and tried to get some rest Nevertheless couldn't. When she finally dozed off she had a dream that she lost the baby to her revenge and woke up screaming. Derrick was by her side instantly telling her it was all a dream. After she calm down and looked around her room to find nothing but flowers and balloons. Oh, baby you didn't have to do this, but I love it though. Derrick was looking serious when he told her they need to talk. Tashione had an idea what the subject would be and was ready to defend herself and reasons. Derrick grabbed Tashione hand and said I love you in unconditionally, I want you to be my wife. Will you marry me? Tashione was really quiet for a minute; then she looked at Derrick and told

him I love you and yes I will be your wife. He palmed her face and sealed it with a kiss. Derrick was so happy he started yelling in addition, the nurses came running in the room. One nurse asked what is all the commotion about? Derrick said we are getting married! Every nurse in the room said congratulations. Tashione wasn't smiling anymore and her revenge was taking over. The nurse left and Derrick sat on the bed and held Tashione in his arms. He told her the wedding plans should keep your mind off revenge now. Tashione tensed up in his arms and said what make you think I'm wanting revenge! She got on the defensive side in addition, said not anymore we got the baby to think about. Derrick was not convince but he left it alone. Derrick looked at his watch and said I love you, now get some rest. Tashione waited till he left and reached over to the drawer and pulled out some paper and pen. She started writing their names down on who she was plotting against. Tashione put the tablet down and dosed off to sleep. The door open and a man came in walking towards the Iv and was about to stick a needle in it. Tashione woke up in addition, asked what are you doing? The man got scared and dropped the needle, on his way out a nurse came in. Tashione told her what happen and the nurse found the needle and said I don't understand English that well. Tashione pushed the button for another nurse to come and when they did she told them what happen. They called the police and then the head Doctor on call. Everybody was in Tashione room when Derrick got there asking questions about what happen here. He had Tashione moved to a private room with a body guard to keep watch around the clock. Derrick asked Tashione to describe the man that came in. When she did the description, it didn't match any of the people Derrick had under watch. Someone was paid to do this but who? Derrick had all the tapes sent to the police station to see who the person was that tried to hurt Tashione. When the man came out he walked towards a lady. She just knew that he done what needed to be done. When he reached her and told her that a nurse came in and he didn't get to do it. She slap him calling him a fool. She was furious and cursed him for everything he was worth. She got in her car and reached him a hundred dollar bill before pulling off. Raul received a phone call telling him that the price has been boosted up, he asked where can he pick up the money. The lady voice told him you will get half now and the restwhen the job was done and hung up. Raul knew he had one chance to get her and he was not about to lose it. Diamond came home and seen Raul in a deep thought so she did not say anything to him. She went in her bedroom and took a shower; and when she was done then she went back out there to join Raul. Once she got Raul attention, she started telling him about how she has assholes working for her. Something needs to be done. The Doctor came in Tashione room and told her, that the stuff that was in the needle was heroin mixed with battery acid. She thanked him and he left. Tashione was

on guard all the time now. She was steady plotting her revenge no matter what Derrick said. She needed to get the fuck out of there, before someone did manage to kill her and the baby. Derrick came in and said baby I got everything covered, so you can relax some. The only ones that can come in this room is the doctor, nurse, me, Keith , and Soul. Derrick what if my parents come to see me? I did tell them I was in the hospital. Well then I have to go make some changes now. Tashione just smiled at Derrick, then said okay so what you bring me. He reached down and pulled out her favorite meal and told her to eat up. Tashione was really tired of eating hospital food, that she ate like she was starving. There was a knock at the door in addition, when it open it was Soul and Keith, stopping by to see how Tashione was doing.

They begin to have the conversation about who was going to have what. Keith wanted a girl and Derrick said well I want a junior. Soul and Tashione said well guys you got to wait till we have it. Keith was telling Derrick that the girls can have an ultra-sound to tell what the sex of the baby will be. Tashione looked at Derrick moreover, saying I don't want to know till I have the baby okay. Soul agreed as well and Keith said I want to know as soon as we can. Keith and Derrick was so excited that they wanted to go baby shopping right away. Soul told Keith to come on let's go home, they said their good-byes and left. Tashione told Derrick she wants to live in her house to raise her baby. Derrick told her not until we catch whoever it is that is trying to kill you. Tashione was ready to get the hell out of the hospital, she has been there for two weeks now and nothing is changing. The Doctor came in to check Tashione and the baby out before the shift change. Derrick went to the bathroom and the Doctor hooked up a machine to Tashione stomach and pulled out his stethoscope to listen to the baby heartbeat. When he looked up, he told Tashione that she may be having twins. Twins! She yelled out! Derrick came out with his gun ready; asking what is going on. Tashione told him to put that gun away, and that we are having twins. Derrick told Tashione that two was going to be a handful. She told him well get ready baby. Derrick asked the Doctor was he sure she was having twins in addition, the Doctor told him yes she is. Derrick sat on the bed and said Damn. Tashione told him he could handle it and smiled. Derrick got in the bed and hugged her. The Doctor unhooked the machine and pushed it in the corner and told Tashione he would see her in the morning and left. Derrick told Tashione he loved her and could not wait to make her his wife and he was in this for the long haul twins or not. Tashione told him she was ready to go home now. Derrick told her she still need to take it easy because the babies are still in danger and your leg is still hurt. He got up and made Tashione comfortable and gave her one of her Zane books called Shame on it all. Derrick turned the television to some baseball team play till he dozed off to sleep. Derrick woke up to find Tashione sleeping with the book on her lap, so he moved the book. He kissed her on the forehead and then step out and told the guard that no more visitors will be coming so don't let no one in the room. While Derrick was driving home he was thinking about how close he has gotten to Tashione and how she brought sunshine back in his life. He vow he will never let any harm come to her while he was with her. Derrick had become very protective over her and he loved that feeling. When he pulled up in his drive way the phone was ringing. When he answered, he was out of breath, but he manage a weak hello. The male voice said how is Tashione doing since I beat that ass and shot her in the leg. You is a sick bastard , I will get you for this soon

enough. The man started laughing and told Derrick that he can't protect her forever. Derrick told him that he should fuck with a man instead of a woman. The male voice told him to be careful what he ask for and hung up. Derrick was really pissed off now. He took a shower and tried to relax but couldn't so he put some clothes on and went back to the hospital. He found Tashione sleeping so peaceful so he got in the chair in addition, watched her till he dozed off. Tashione and the Doctor was talking about letting her go home today and she was happy and told the Doctor that she was ready. Once the Doctor left to get the paperwork together Tashione woke up Derrick to tell him the good news. Baby why didn't you wake me up while the Doctor was in here. They waited for the Doctor to bring in the papers, so she could sign them and get the hell out of there. Once the Doctor brought the papers Tashione hurried up and signed them in addition, grabbed Derrick by the hand to leave the room. Derrick stop Tashione and said thank you for all that you have done for us. The Doctor told him to go ahead and take her out of here and don't let her over do it. While driving home Derrick stop by the Chinese Restaurant and ordered all kinds of Tashione favorite foods. When they arrived at the house Tashione was shock to see all kinds of banners and balloons plus flowers. Tashione looked at Derrick and said I love you so much. Oh no, I can't take the credit for this one, and Soul came out of the kitchen with a cake saying welcome home. Derrick and Keith helped Tashione to the conch and started passing out plates. Soul cut on some music and, they all ate together talking and laughing about baby names. Once they was done eating Soul cleaned up some and they left. Derrick asked Tashione was she ready to go to bed and she told him yes. He picked her up and carried her upstairs. He cut on the television and Buffy was on; he was about to turn it when she told him not to because she liked the show. They laid in the bed and Derrick told Tashione that if she don't slow down in eating that she was going to be big as a house. I don't see shit funny Derrick! Derrick tried to stop laughing nevertheless, it was really hard because Tashione was pouting. He did tell her that if she could not wash her body and her fat swollenfeet that he promise he would. The telephone started ringing and it was Soul calling asking her to stand up in her wedding. Soul why don't we have a double wedding ! Derrick just smiled. He was happy now and he had the best thing that could ever happen to him in his life. Listen girl we can talk about this in the morning because I am really tired. Okay girl and I can't wait. Derrick put his shorts on and laid next to her. Tashione was feeling horney, and wanted to have sex so she started kissing Derrick on the neck. He asked her was it okay to make love? Yes baby! So give up the goods. He climb on top and caressed her legs and Tashione moan. Derrick started tongue kissing her; then she palmed his ass to let him know she wanted to fuck. He lift her nightgown and kissed her body all over and down to her clit. He told her to stay still so she won't hurt her leg. He open her lips and her clit was visible and he begin to suck and caress. Tashione palm his head and started grinding her pussy against him. He got up and slide his dick in her, gradually moving slow at first. Tashione was very hot and she wanted it faster. She asked Derrick are you going to play with me or fuck me. He picked up his pace and after a few minutes he was nutting and so was she. They fell asleep in each other arms. A couple of months went by and nothing happen. Soul called Tashione up and asked did she want to go shopping for the babies. Tashione said yeah girl, however, I have a Doctor appointment at 10:00. I tell you

what when I am done I will call you to let you know I'm on my way. Soul said okay and hung up. Derrick was in the kitchen cooking breakfast and the smell made Tashione sick on her stomach. She ran to the bathroom and shit went every where. Derrick was calling her name, but she couldn't answer for throwing up. When he walked in the bathroom and grabbed a washcloth and ran cold water on it. Tashione was just heaving now and nothing was coming up. Derrick wipe her face and picked her up then laid her in the bed. Tashione told Derrick I can't keep nothing down; any smell of food makes me sick . Oh Derrick what am I going to do? I got to eat though. Derrick apologized and helped her get ready for the doctor appointment. Once there they waited 45 minutes before her name was called. Back in the room she had to undress and sit on the table to wait for the doctor to come in. Ten minutes came and there was a knock on the door before it was open. The doctor introduced herself as Ms. Rogers; while reaching for some gloves to put on. She asked Derrick was he the father; well it is so good to see that you are here. She told Tashione what she was going to do and then did the exam. Ms. Rogers asked Tashione did she know she was having twins. Tashione said yes we do, but how are the babies doing because they had weak heartbeats due to an accident I had. Yes, I have copy of your record from the hospital and the heart rate are fine. I'm going to draw blood and do a ultra-sound in just a few minutes. She asked them did they want to see their babies? Derrick was yelling yes, but Tashione said I don't want to know the sex either. The doctor stepped out and Derrick was a little upset, because he really wanted to know even if she didn't. The doctor came back in and squirt some jelly on her stomach and ran this piece over her stomach to show the babies. She showed them the babies head ,legs, spine. Tashione had tears in her eyes now and could not believe she was having kids after all these years. The doctor went on and looked at the sex just in case they changed their mind but didn't say a word. Dr. Rogers asked Tashione was she taking her prenatal vitamins and eating healthy foods. Yes, but the smell of food makes me sick on my stomach. I do have this weird craving for Argo starch. Oh no, Tashione you can't eat that. It's not healthy and it will clog you up. Dr. Rogers told her she was done and to get dress. Once Tashione was dress, they went to the check out counter for her next appointment. Derrick told Tashione that he forgot his keys and went back to the room. He seen Dr. Rogers and asked her what can he do to help Tashione with her morning sickness. The doctor told him that it was normal and would pass soon enough. Um one more thing Doctor can you tell me what the sex is of our babies. Yes, she is having a boy and a girl. Oh, thank you so much and I know Tashione don't want to know so can you keep this between us. Derrick went back out to meet Tashione and they got in the car heading for the police station. When she dropped him off she told him that she was going shopping with Soul and could he catch a ride with Keith home. Of course, baby, he kissed her and he walked off. Tashione called Soul and told her to be ready when she got there. When Tashione arrived she blew the horn and Soul came out. Once on the road Soul told Tashione to go to Baby's

World, girl can you believe we are pregnant at the same time. Who would have ever guess that I would be pregnant again, Tashione said. When they got in the store, they seen so many pretty things that one went one way and the other a different way. Tashione was at the cribs and seen two cribs that was white and it had a place where you could put the baby name. She wrote down the item number and price, then she went to the area that held all the

accessories for the crib. She was writing down more information. Then she went and got baby bottles and diaper and nursing kit. Tashione said she wouldn't buy any clothes until later on. By the time she caught up with Soul, they were ready to go to check out. They made sure everything would be shipped in one week. Soul asked Tashione do she want to go unwind at the Olive Garden. Yeah girl, we can do that. Once inside the waiter came over asking what would they like to drink. Both woman said a glass of red wine please. The waiter set two menu down for them to look at while he was gone. The waiter could not believe his luck and made a phone call saying both girls are here eating lunch. The other male voice told him to make sure that they did not leave until he got there and hung up.

When the waiter came back he had a bottle of red wine and poured the ladies a glass then asked was they ready to order. Both ladies told what they wanted to eat and he walked off. By this time, another waiter was leading Raul toward their table. Soul told Tashione that Raul was here and that she was ready to leave. The ladies didn't even eat their food and paid for the everything. They left without Raul even seeing them. Raul called Diamond and told them that Tashione was at the Olive Garden and to meet him there and hung up. The waiter came over to Raul table and told him that the ladies are gone and don't know how long they have been gone. Raul was pissed off and he called Diamond back to cancel but got no answer. Raul knew something spooked them because they would have

never left. When Diamond got there she was like what's up baby. Nothing much I just wanted to take you out for lunch that is all. Oh, Raul that is so sweet of you and she leans over to kiss him. Tashione and Soul was still hungry as hell so they just got them a sub sandwich and went to Derrick house. Soul do you know that I did not get sick when we was in the Olive Garden. Well you know what that mean right? I sure do and it's on tomorrow, are you down girl. Of course I am;call me when you is ready. The next day Tashione and Soul was on their way back to the Olive Garden to eat and the same waiter seated them. They ordered the same thing and this time the waiter put the visine in their wine and watched them drink it all up. And even refill their glass while they ate dinner. The waiter called Raul and told him they was back and would not be leaving this time. I want you to park your car at the back door. Once everything was done Tashione and Soul seen Raul standing there with this big ass smile on his face. Neither women can say anything, then pass out. Raul motion for the waiter to come over and help him get the woman to his car. Raul said put their asses in the trunk then drives off. Once he got to Tashione house he put Soul on the bed and stripes her of her clothes and then blindfold her. He goes back to the car and get Tashione. Raul was mumbling to himself about how heavy Tashione ass has gotten since she was pregnant. He takes her to their old bedroom and lay her down on the bed and tie her hands and legs to the bedpost. He cut Tashione clothes off her and begin to touch and caress her nipples. He then take his hand and spread her pussy lips apart to where he sees her clit. And then take his tongue and go across it several times. Raul notice that his dick was harder by the minute. He put his dick in Tashione and fucked her as hard as he could while she was out cold. He bust his nut and his dick still didn't go down, he knew it would be that way with Tashione.Because that was the kind of effect, she had on him. He get up and go in the room where Soul is and say I always wanted to fuck your high and mighty ass and now I have the chance too. He lift her ass up and slowly stroke her. Raul is grunting and pulls out and nut on her chest. Raul cell phone was going off and when he answered it was a male voice asking where is she. Raul said I won't say over the phone but if you think about long enough I'm close to you now bye. Thirty minutes went by and the man that Raul was talking too was coming through the door. Therefore, what are we going to do with them now? Hell I don't even know yet. Well let me crave the baby out of this one before I slit her throat. Man you are really a sick bastard and started laughing. Listen do not touch them I got some calls to make first. Raul left and went to a pay phone and called Derrick house which he got the answering machine. He told Derrick that he could not always protect Tashione that he had her and Soul then hung up. Derrick and

Keith have been trying to call the girls all day; and could not get an answer so they decided to go to the house. Once they got there, nobody was there and Keith noticed that light was blinking on the machine and told Derrick about it. Derrick went to the machine and hit the button and when they heard the message they both freaked the fuck out. Derrick and Keith knew who it was and went to the police station to get an warrant for them. Once they got it they had to figure out where he was holding the girls. They sent men to Brian apartment to pick his ass up but no one was there. They got a call that Tashione car was at the Olive Garden on Main Street. Once they got there and went to the police Officer, who made it there first to see if he found something. The police officer told him that he found keys and a note saying you will never make it in time to save that bitch. The manager told Derrick that the car was here when I came on shift and was still here, an hour before my shift end. I thought someone was planning to rob us that is why I called. Keith thanked the man and turned to Derrick who was thinking really hard. Derrick looked at Keith and said I know where they are and lets go. Keith wanted to know and kept asking where man. Derrick said Tashione house I bet, no one went there and that is the perfect place to kill her in her own home. Keith told Derrick to step on it. Once they got a block away they headed out on foot. By the time they reached the house they could hear the ladies screaming for help. Keith told Derrick to split up and they do. Raul and the man are laughing and screaming right along with the ladies because they just know no one will come to their aid. The man asked Tashione are you comfortable? She asked him who he was because this is wrong to help Raul kill her. Well lady right now that is not important, but I will tell you before I kill you. Tashione flinched as the man rubbed her titties. He told her if she screamed or yell he would slice her throat. Tashione was begging him to please let her go because she was pregnant. Raul heard this and ran over to her and said you bitch and slaps her. Tashione then recognized Raul voice and started to put everything together now. Tashione begins to scream on Raul now asking him why is he doing this. Raul slaps her again and toldthe man to gag that bitch for I kill her now.

CHAPTER 20

Once the man gagged her and she was quiet Raul begin to tell her why he was doing this to her. Tashione could not believe what she was hearing and Derrick heard it all too, however, kept his presence silent and hope Keith got Soul out like he said. Raul tells the man to stand aside and watchedhim fuck this bitch. Tashione was trying to get away but couldn't and Raul begin to finger fuck her. Tashione felt helpless but the rage was building up stronger and stronger. Raul took his shoes off and dropped his pants and boxers. Climb on top and lift her ass up so he can ram his dick into her. Raul had already let her know that he fucked and sucked her once already while she was out cold. He even told her that is was better when she was out cold. The

man was laughing now but he heard Soul so he went to check on her. She was still tied up on the bed and he told her to shut her fucking mouth before he sticks something in it. As a matter of fact you can put this dick in your mouth. If you even think about biting my shit I will kill you; just think about that baby you is carrying. Soul begin to quiet down and sucked the man dick, he must have felt the change because he told her no funny business or you are dead. Soul felt his muscle tighten up and knew he was going to pull out; but he didn't and she felt his warm cum hitting the back of her throat. When he pulled out Soul swallowed and asked him could she get her pussy sucked in return. He told her why not since it will be your last. He went down to eat her pussy and Soul said; oh hell no! stop licking my pussy like a kitten does a bowl of milk. Man you got to get down and up in the pussy, tongue kiss that motherfucker. Soul had to tell him don't suck it till it's sore and sensitive. How about sliding your dick in this good hot pussy. Brian was all for it. Soul was baiting his ass up , so she can do something to get free. Brian was fucking Soul like he was dogs in heat. Soul had to stop him and said look baby I want you to slow down your strokes. Then I want you to learn how to make love to a woman before you kill me. Brian did just what Soul said. She had him fucking her titties and even the 69 which he loved the best. She was ready to try her luck now and asked him to untie her hands, so she could show him more ways. Brian got off the bed in addition, locked the door then he unloaded the gun. He walked over to the bed and untied her, but he kept one leg tied but loosens it up. He flips her and she was on her knees, with her ass up in the air. Brian said, now that's what's up! Soul told him she wanted to see what he could do with all this ass in front of him. He spread her ass cheeks and slide the tip of his dick in and Soul screamed out, but not in pain. Keith heard the screams and he couldn't get to her right yet without getting her killed. Brian stop, and Soul told him to keep going baby I love this shit. Brian couldn't believe this shit he was hearing and bust a nut in her ass. His dick was going down now in addition, he still wanted to know more. Soul told Brian to lay down and she will make him rise again. Raul was tired of fucking Tashione because she wouldn't move. He asked Tashione what's wrong bitch you don't like it no more? Raul pulls out his dick and begins to hit her across the face with it. He still wasn't getting a reaction from her and now he was getting pissed. Raul put her nipples in his mouth but still nothing, so he moves down to the pussy and lick across her lips. Tashione just turned her head to the side and started crying. She started to remember how it felt to be helpless and vowed to herself that she will kill Raul herself. Raul slide his finger in the pussy and started hitting the g-spot; and Tashione gasp out loud. Raul said, that's right baby you know papi` know all your spots. Tashione got wetter and she almost climax till she bit her lip. Raul said as long as you don't let me taste your cum I will keep teasing it till you do.

Now bitch what it is going to be! She just looked at him with pure hatred in her eyes. He went back to sucking her pussy and he fingered her ass. That brought Tashione up off the bed some. Raul smiles and hum on her clit. Tashione just gave up the fight so she could get him the fuck off her so she faked a nut. She even went all out to make him feel like she was enjoying it. At first Raul was falling for it till she called out his name, that brought back the why he even had her there in the first place. Brian learned so much from Soul that he want her to make him rise so she could suck him off again. Brian went to tie Soul hands back up, but she kicked him so hard in his dick that he fell over screaming. Soul tried to get loose and she did just in time, because Brian was about to get to his feet. When she ran out the door buck ass naked she ran into Keith. She went to swinging her arms and Keith told her it's okay he got her now. Soul calmed down some and he told her to go find some clothes and go get in the car. Brian was calling for Raul now but when the door open up it was Keith looking at him like he could kill him. Derrick checked his gun and now was at the bedroom door waiting for his chance and when he heard movement he rushed in pointing his gun at Raul. Raul is nervous as hell in addition, tried to grab his gun but Tashione made him fall short. Derrick told him to freeze and he did. Derrick made Raul lay down face down with his hands on his head so he could cuff him. Derrick then goes and untie Tashione and hugged her real tight. Raul now says Oh look the savior has arrived and started laughing. Tashione goes to her closet in addition, get her short hand 9mm and cocks it. She needed to feel safe and that helped her out a lot. Derrick grabs Raul by the arm to lift him up and take him downstairs and read him his rights. Keith already had Brian ass sitting on the conch waiting. When Derrick went to uncuff Raul so he could cuff him to his brother; Raul pushed Derrick back and gets his gun he had on his calf. Derrick hear Tashione voice and Raul scream out you bitch and went to fire his gun which caught Derrick in the chest. Keith is now struggling with Brian and the gun goes off and he falls as well. Tashione is holding Derrick in her arms begging him not to leave her. Derrick the babies need their father and I need you. Keith use his cell phone to call for back up and Raul is now pointing the gun at Tashione in addition, she stands up and point hers at him. Brian crawls over to Raul and pull on his leg; and took Raul attention away from Tashione for a few seconds to many and she opens fire on his ass. Tashione unloaded the gun in Raul. The back up got there to see Tashione open fire on Raul and kill him in a malicious way. Keith told one police officer that they had a man down and need to get him to the hospital. Soul runs in the house with a blanket on and runs into Keith arms. Tashione is now at Derrick side telling him to hold on for her and the kids. Derrick looked up and asked her how are the babies doing and cough. The ambulance came and they put Derrick on the structure and Tashione was left there looking at Raul dead body. Tashione went to walk pass and Keith pulled the trigger, and his shot went wild and Tashione shot Brian in his arm. The other police officer comes in and to get Brian and someone else put Raul body in a body bag. Everybody is at the hospital now. Derrick is in surgery and Soul and Tashione was being checked out because they both were carrying babies. Once they got a clean bill of health, they rushed to where Keith was at. Soul asked Keith can she go see Brian? He looked at her then asked are you sure you want to do this. Yes baby I am; because I want him to see the pain and hurt he caused me. Keith leads her to Brian room and she goes in. Brian is just looking at the ceiling in a daze. Soul see that he is handcuffed to the bed rail and he couldn't get to her any more. Soul call Brian name and then asked him why did he do this? Brian had this crazy look on his face and said that bitch killed my brother. He also told Soul he would never have killed her because he loved her. Soul told him that he was a sick man and she hopes he riot in hell. She leaves the room and Keith is there to comfort her in his arms. All three of them are waiting to hear how Derrick is doing. A tall slender woman dressed in a nurse uniform goes to Brian room and when he see her he went to call out her name. Two shot to the head and one to the chest leaving him forming the woman name on his lips. She leaves out without anyone even second-guessing her identity.

THE END

COMING SOON "A Heart's Desire"

PART 2

JACQUELINE CUNNINGHAM is a graduate from York Technical College with an Associate Degree in Science. Born in Brooklyn New York and moving to South Carolina where she is raising her children.

Printed in the United States
by Baker & Taylor Publisher Services